Copyright © 2024 by Jennifer Lauer

Library of Congress Control Number: 2024947218

All rights reserved.

No part of this book may be reproduced in any form or by any electronic or mechanical means, including information storage and retrieval systems, without written permission from the author, except for the use of brief quotations in a book review.

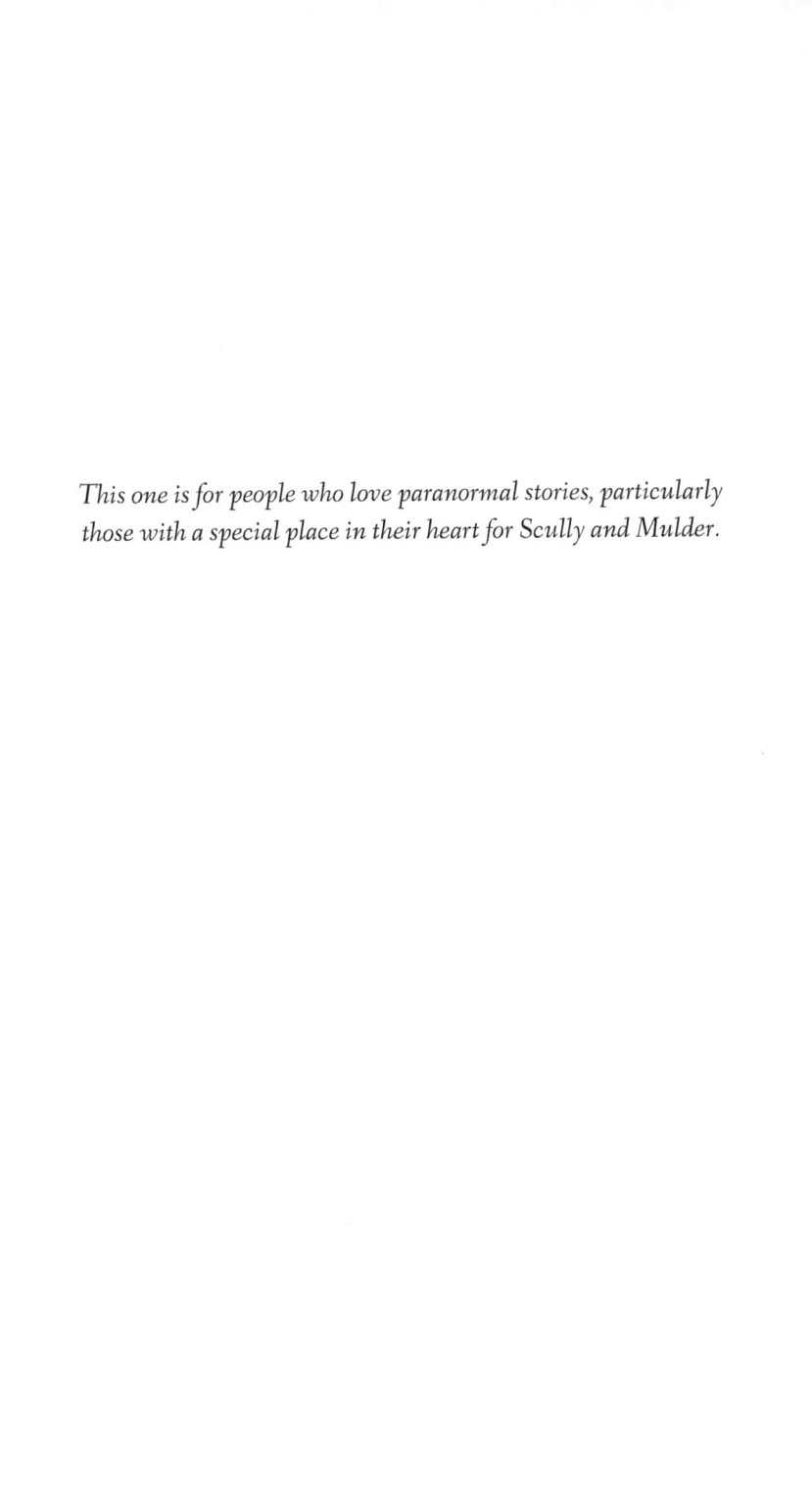

This one is for people who love paranormal stories, particularly those with a special place in their heart for Scully and Mulder.

START SOMEWHERE
THE STRANGE CHRONICLES
BOOK 1

JENNIFER LAUER

1

Have you ever wondered what the world would feel like without a mother? I never did.

But this is my new reality.

One week ago, my beloved mother was killed in a fire. We held her funeral earlier today, and everyone has left but me. I know I should leave too.

My heart is empty now. The darkness of night feels oppressive, as I look to my watch to check the time – midnight.

Time to go.

The night is cool, as September is in Massachusetts, and I can't stay here forever, even if that is exactly what I want to do. After one last rearrangement of the flowerpots at the foot of the bench, I use the sleeve of my coat to polish the brass plate on the seat that reads, *In Loving Memory of Madeline Cooper*.

The bench is a kind gesture from the Wildlife Reserve at Sandy Point. My mother had worked for them for the last thirty years, and the bench overlooks the ocean. The director received special permission to have a bench placed here in her honor. The ceremony was lovely, something I imagine Mom would've come home and told me about if she had been a guest.

But she wasn't.

Because she isn't here anymore.

Mom is gone.

The pressure around my heart crushes inward just a small bit more, even though I can't imagine there is any space left.

The funeral was a small gathering of friends, family, and coworkers. A friend from the Reserve, Patty, had brought birdseed. We tossed it about to attract the sea birds. Two double-crested cormorants showed up. They were Mom's favorite. It felt as though they came to pay their respects.

During the ceremony, I'd managed the strength to read a small passage from Walden and was quite relieved I'd chosen such a short one, because the ache in my throat made it difficult to form words.

Celebrating by the water felt cleansing and nourishing, after the tragic way she had left.

Today has been the longest day I've ever lived, and the reality of having to drive home to Salem exhausts me.

When I get to my pristine, electric '68 Nova, who I call Hero, I rest my hand on the driver's side window and take a breath to steady myself before getting in. Staying here longer is not going to bring her back.

It's only an hour's drive, but the long dark highway only intensifies the loneliness.

Somehow a world without a mother feels bigger, which in turn makes me feel smaller.

Flipping on my Comforting Classical playlist, I spot the little red dot of a voicemail notification on my phone. Hitting Play, I inhale deeply at the expectation of whatever platitudes are about to be unleashed.

Instead, I hear the surprising gruffness of an unfamiliar voice.

"Hiya, Ms. Cooper, this is Joe. Joe Nebraska, Mistwell Insurance. So, I have the case file here on a Madeline Cooper. I'm sorry for your loss. Calling to let you know we've denied the claim. Unfortunately, you are not entitled to the death benefits, due to the policyholder's cause of death ... which the investigation showed to be suicide. If you have any questions, my secretary Blake will take care of you. Thank you for choosing Mistwell," Joe says and then ... *click.*

I steer hard into the breakdown lane.

"Impossible," I say to no one, and rest my head onto the steering wheel to cry.

This is not right.

There's no way this is true.

How could they have it so wrong? This insurance company, they must've made a mistake, mixed up their files or something.

And the nerve of some low-rate insurance salesman to call me on the day of my mother's funeral to give me this false information. He doesn't know me, and he certainly didn't know my mother.

Madeline Cooper would never, could never...

I won't finish the thought because it hurts too much. A heavy weight burrows into my chest. Not only am I surprised, but the budding of a new feeling is taking hold.

Betrayal.

Is it possible?

Could my punchy, no-nonsense mother, with plans and responsibilities and absolutely no signs of depression, just suddenly have given up?

I'd been under the impression that mom's death was a

tragic accident, caused by faulty wiring in the wall of her house. The fire department had been quite certain.

Something did not add up.

I have tried to disassociate from my mother's case.

This is not work.

Her case is not the thing I've been training for; she is my own blood.

My mother.

I'm allowing myself the grace to fall apart, without allowing any of my investigative knowledge to edge its way into my mind.

Even when the fire chief looked distracted that night and when I noticed the new dishes in Mom's cabinets, I kept myself focused on my own grief. Even when I came back to the house the next day and saw ashen footsteps on the stone path leading to the backyard shed.

I chalked the footsteps up to having been left by the fire investigators, and I didn't check the shed.

How could I have let that all go?

Mistwell Insurance has no idea what they just started. I will make sure they correct their mistake and apologize. I'm not some pedestrian—I'm Gray Cooper, Private Detective. Technically, this is true, even if I haven't officially referred to myself as a gumshoe in any public way.

Yet.

And the other bit I hardly want to acknowledge is the money. Without the life insurance money, there's no way of paying the remaining bills, not to mention dealing with every other loose end my mom has left me.

Intent on starting my own business, I have gone so far as getting a tax ID and setting up an LLC.

But now that Mom's dead, I've pressed Stop on my life.

I've put the idea of being a PI away, tucked it into a drawer until later when dealing with real life can happen again.

Regret swallows me.

I looked out the windshield into the black night. The sound of crickets comes to a crescendo, and then stops.

Silence.

"I didn't kill myself, you know," Mom says, matter-of-factly. My nerves nearly shake out of my body.

I look over at the passenger seat, to see my mother staring into the flipped down sun visor, eyeballing herself in the mirror.

My hands shake as I rub my eyes, as if to rub away the image, but when I look again, she is still there.

Mom. Madeline.

This is not real.

This is not real.

"Mom?" I ask, my heart feeling both shattered and warm at the same time.

"Good God, Gray, I don't have a reflection," she says. She stares at the visor, looking bewildered.

"That's because you're dead," I respond. I reach out to touch my mother's arm, but my hand goes right through her and lands on the leather armrest. I let out a disappointed sigh.

Tears flood my eyes. I want her to be here so much. But she's not, she can't be. It's my mind playing a cruel trick.

"Oh, darling, don't be so drab. Tell that Joe Nebraska guy to write the check. You most certainly *will* be getting my life insurance, I did not pay that premium for years to have you suffer," she says as she turns to face me.

What? I must have completely and totally lost my mind. I'm hallucinating. My hands are shaking. She seems so real. Her voice...

"Call him," she says.

"What would I say to him if I call? '*Hello, sir, my mom did not kill herself. She told me so,*'" I say to my mom.

I look down at my phone where the Mistwell Insurance phone number sits at the top of my recent calls. I will need to call him and deal with their botched investigation. Even if she's just in my head, I have to ask, "Mom, what happened, with the fire?"

But as I look up from the phone, I find that my mother has left me.

Again.

2

When I got home last night, I fell asleep in my clothes. I did not sleep well. Now the aching morning sun makes me squint. I'm still working out how to explain to this insurance guy that my mother did not kill herself. I'm hoping they'll recognize their mistake and I won't have to explain a thing.

After I put on some clothes and brush my teeth, I check the address and head straight there.

Only a few cars are in the parking lot, and the office building is shabbier than I expected. It's certainly possible their "claim investigators" aren't top shelf. The smudged glass door reads *MISTWELL INS.* and as I push through, a sad bell rings.

A young man in a black hoodie sits at the front desk, eating a sleeve of Oreos. It is clear whatever game he's playing on his computer is more exciting than helping me.

"Excuse me. Excuse *me*," I say, trying to get his attention in vain. When he doesn't look up from his screen, and I see a partial headphone covered by his hoodie. Annoyed, I turn and go back to the door and slam it closed again.

And again, the sad bell rings.

"Oh, uh, can I help you?" the clueless man says, pulling one side of the headphones off.

"I am here to see Joe Nebraska." I'm firm, trying to keep the dragon's fire inside my head from singeing the place.

"Joe!" he shouts. "Hey, Joe, some lady for ya!"

"I'm not some lady, I'm..." I try to explain but am interrupted by the smooth entrance of a man in a collared shirt, sleeves rolled to the elbows. He has the shadow of a beard, and a ruddy complexion, likely from spending too much time in the sun. Not sure where he'd found so much sun, being that it's autumn in Massachusetts.

"Gray Cooper, I suppose?" he asks with more curiosity than bother.

"Yes, are you Joe? I received your phone message," I say, noticing that my heart adds a beat.

"I'm as Joe as I could be. Blake, get Ms. Cooper some coffee. You can follow me this way," Joe says with an ease that makes me angry, as he pushes a lock of dark hair behind his ear.

"I don't want coffee," I scoffed, even though I do. I can feel the remnants of last night's wretched sleep.

Joe stands behind a messy desk piled with files and paperwork, and gestures for me to sit. A door to the left, presumably a bathroom, has a sign reading *WASH YOUR HANDS – SERIOUSLY*. He seems like a paradox – a messy germaphobe? A weathered leather jacket hangs from his chair. I wait for him to sit before I do.

This Joe is so unlikable, telling me when to sit, ordering coffee I didn't ask for. This is the kind of guy I always stay far away from – his high cheekbones and warm, deep voice do nothing to help.

"So, about this sham investigation that told you geniuses my mother killed herself," I start. I'm mad and can't hide it.

"Easy, Ms. Cooper," he says. Another instruction.

"No. I won't take it easy. You are going to go over every bit of information with me in profound detail, and I will show you every single mistake you made, and then you will apologize in tears as you sign a check, begging me not to sue you," I threaten.

I straighten the sturdy wool jacket I've tossed on over my barely ironed top. Joe throws me a confident smile, and we lock eyes. Joe's eyes are slate, like cloud cover masking previous storms, and looking into them makes something inside me soften.

"Gray Cooper, you are something else," he says, as he lifts folders looking for something.

"I don't play games, Mr. Nebraska," I say, wondering if that is his real name.

"Joe, please. And I can see that. What do you do?" he asks.

"What do you mean?" I'm suspect.

"Your job, besides finessing the likes of me," he asks in an old-timey way that annoys me.

"I'm a private investigator," I say quietly, which isn't exactly true.

"I see, so you think you know better than our investigators?" he asks genuinely.

"I'm saying I know my mother better than your investigators, yes," I say, slowly standing up. "I want to know how they came to the conclusion of suicide."

I can't help my voice lilting up an octave.

"They found this." He rummages in a drawer and pulls out a folder and takes out a Ziploc holding a singed paper inside, which he hands to me.

The top portion is burned off, but the remaining bit is certainly my mother's smooth cursive.

...I'm sorry, this wasn't how I wanted it to end. Please forgive me. I've messed things up badly, and so I suppose it's apropos that it all goes up in flames.

All my love, Mads

It's jarring to see her words. So delicately penned, saying such urgent things. I can see how this looks bad. And Mads? Who had ever called my mother Mads? No one, to my knowledge.

I slip the bag with the note into my purse, rising to go, hoping to blink away the tears brimming my eyes.

"You can't take that," Joe says.

"The letter is not as definitive as you think," I say. Ignoring him, I turn and leave, pushing out of his office.

His chair scratches the floor, as he stands up.

Charging past the front desk with an empty chair, no hoodied Blake in my way, I half-think Joe will come chasing after me. I grab at the door handle and glance back, to see Joe leaning in his office doorway, watching me leave with a defeated grin.

Once I get to the car, I dial George, the man my mom had been seeing for the last five or so years. I like George well enough, even though his sense of humor errs on the side of obvious puns. Oh, did he make mom laugh. The more tragically unfunny George's puns were, the harder she would laugh.

"Hi, George, it's Gray," I say, as he picks up right away. "I have sort of a strange question for you – did you happen to call mom, 'Mads'?" I know my question seems abrupt and out of context, but there isn't time for explanations and pleasantries.

When I hear his response, I purse my lips firmly.

"Thank you, George. No, no it's just a mistake, I think. Sorry to bother you. Dinner? Yes, of course, tomorrow works just fine. Okay. See you then."

I end the call.

If George didn't call my mother 'Mads,' and I never have, then the letter could not be a suicide note. There is no way Madeline Cooper would have left her last words to anyone but me or George. Unless there is someone I don't know about, but I shake the thought from my mind.

There is work to do. I must find out who this letter is for, and what it means.

3

After a long day of chasing my tail with dead-end leads and no answer from the fire chief, I make my way to my father's office. Winding down the woodsy lane, the telephone poles flicker past. The stone gravestones begin to appear on my right-hand side. And I slow, to take the left turn by the oversized gargoyle marking the end of the cemetery. As I move, Hero's lights illuminate the deviled face, it's gothic horns and stone wings tucked behind its body. Even though I've seen it hundreds of times, the stone eyes follow me like the Mona Lisa effect, and a chill crawls up my neck.

When I arrive at the small office park, the lot is empty, and if I weren't so tired, it might be spooky.

I can't help looking over at the passenger seat, hoping Mom will reappear, but the sad truth of nothingness stares back at me.

It couldn't have been real.

I'm delirious with grief.

Get it together, Gray.

It has been years since I've been inside my father's office, but I hope surrounding myself with his things, his case files, maybe his presence will bring me some answers.

My father, Woody Cooper, was a PI. He worked "strange cases." Well, that's how he and Mom put it. He disappeared ten years ago, while working a case. It was as though a switch had flipped and he vanished. Then Mom got news of his death, and we were both devasted. I was twenty-two. All I remember is staring down at my mismatched Converse, one red, one blue. I stared and stared until my eyes crossed and the colors combined into a violet hue.

The key, which I haven't used until now, works easily. The familiar musty smell of old paper and wood and honey hits me with a shock of nostalgia. The place is cluttered with case files, books and mugs.

My father had been a broad collector of coffee mugs – large Christmas mugs, tiny European mugs, glass, wooden, you name it. And he did not display them in a glass case for special viewing; instead they collected dust in the near and far reaches of his office.

Sitting with my notebook, preferring a pen and pad to the digital version, I sink into my father's, cozy, tan leather chair, which had molded to the shape of him. I intend to make a list of my 'to-do's', but I started to nod off.

No.

I shake myself awake.

Must stay awake and figure out what happened to my mother. And so, despite the late hour, I get up and find the coffee maker. Never have I been so grateful to find the last dregs of dark roast left in a bag in the door of the unplugged minifridge. Probably stale, but it's not moldy.

After making just a cup's worth, I grab the pot early, carelessly. While it's still brewing, coffee leaks all over and sizzles when I return the pot to the burner.

I drink it too hot to taste, and look out the smudged window, allowing my gaze to soften and settle in between awake and asleep.

The phone rings.

It's an old-fashioned ring tone that I can't place. Then I remembered – a landline. Mom had some bills for it at the house; strange that she'd keep it in service after Dad's death. Everyone grieves differently.

Searching on shelves and along the walls, I find the beige phone underneath paperwork on the desk.

"Hello," I say, internally cursing myself for answering at all.

"Is this Detective Cooper?" a nervous voice asks.

No. Not me. Detective Cooper was Dad. But I got my certificate six months ago, and so I suppose I am Detective Cooper too.

"Private Investigator, yes. Cooper, that's me. How can I help you?" I rub my hand on the side of my jeans, trying to push the nerves out.

"My name is Darby Vondale, and I need some help with my grandfather. He went missing last night and my family is kind of … well, I found this card with your number and thought you could help," she says.

Wow. A missing persons case. It's everything I've trained for, and it found me with my life in shambles.

"I'm sorry, I'm not really taking any new cases right now," I say, not mentioning that I've never taken any case ever before.

"Please, we have money. He left without his wallet or keys. He's not mental, something happened to him. Please." The desperation in her voice is relatable. And, I'll admit, the mention of money perks my ears embarrassingly, like a puppy spotting a squirrel out the window.

"I don't think so. Can't you just leave it to the police?" I say, because taking this case would be impossible right now.

"They're useless, they think he's a geriatric case wandering off with dementia, but he's not. They are checking hospitals, please, if you could just come and take a look around his room, maybe outside, maybe you'll see something we don't?" Darby's voice cracks.

There is no way to accommodate this poor woman, but I can't help feeling sorry for her. That's what happened with my dad. I have known the agony of a family member disappearing without explanation, and I know how important the first few hours of the investigation are.

"Okay, I will come by tomorrow, but I can't promise anything and I'm definitely not taking the case. I'll see if there is anything glaring the police could have missed," I say.

"Thank you, thank you, Ms. Cooper. I really appreciate it. We are at 526 Thornball Road. Does noon work?" Darby asks.

"Yes, I'll be there at noon," I say.

"Great. Oh, and just an fyi – my family will be there, and they are ... a handful." And with that Darby hangs up.

Looking down at my half full coffee mug, I take a long, deep breath. I need the money. Without Mom's life insurance and any other job I'm qualified for, I have to take it.

At the same time, I wonder, why do I always insist on adding layers of difficulty to my life, when things are already at the tipping point?

4

As I turn up Thornball Road, to the Vondale house, I wonder what kind of "handful" I am walking into. Weird or stressful enough for Darby to warn me. It couldn't be worse than the Cooper family drama.

This is it; I'm following in Dad's footsteps – it's both terrifying and electrifying. Although, I don't have many memories of his cases, I remember his joy and sometimes his sadness. He wasn't treated well by some colleagues or taken seriously.

I pull Hero in behind the self-driver in the gravel driveway.

Checking my device, I have messages. One from Lucy, whom I haven't called since the night my mother died. Lucy is a friend from detective school, but we had a falling out because I missed her wedding, and then solidified our separation by not responding to her calls about Mom's funeral.

Another from Gramma Sugar who I can't call back, because well, she's my father's mother. Although, I count her as my closest confidant, I've had a difficult time discussing anything to do with my father since we were informed of his death.

Make a mental note to call them both as soon as I am finished. Now is not the time to alienate those closest to me.

The Vondale house is enormous. Four white pillars hold up the front porch and a gold lion knocker on the front door gives the place horror-movie vibes.

Old money.

I grab my locksmith set and pepper spray and put them in my inner trench pocket, only because I always do, not because I'm expecting to use them.

Slip my hand into my other pocket to retrieve some cinnamon candy as I knock on the door. I love the way the heat makes my mouth tingle, and it helps me focus.

As though she were waiting just behind the door, Darby Vondale pops out immediately. Her big red curls bounce as she smiles, revealing bright white teeth, and she shakes my hand with too much enthusiasm. She wears a simple beige cashmere sweater.

"Ms. Cooper, thank you so much. I'm so glad you are here, can I take your coat?" Darby says.

"I'll keep it, thanks," I say as I sling my coat over my arm and enter. Darby nods and ushers me inside, where a football game blares from the television.

Two men sit in the living room cheering heartily, but when Darby peeks her head into the room, their faces sour. Noteworthy.

"Barry, Gerald, this is Gray Cooper," she says.

Barry, who looks to be in his late thirties, gives a small wave, his blue ballcap is printed with *BARRY*, and he strokes his mustache with his index finger. I notice he holds his other hand over his left pocket, which is likely where he keeps his wallet. Something about the presence of a woman makes Barry worry about his money.

He is exactly why I've sworn off relationships.

Gerald, the other guy, is fortyish. He wears untied boat shoes and a university fleece, and gives an acknowledging nod. Both have pale, smooth hands, like they've never handled anything sharper than a touchscreen. I get the feeling my presence is neither welcome nor invited.

"Just ignore them, my brothers are self-involved jerks," Darby says. I do not ignore them, even if I do agree with the insulting characterization.

"My mother, Misty and sister Caroline, are outside in the garden," Darby explains as I followed her through the house of shining hardwood floors adorned with vibrant wool rugs. Darby pushes through French doors to reveal Misty and Caroline Vondale sitting at a cast-iron table, both with phones out and folders in stacks around them.

"Mother, this is Gray Cooper, the detective I told you about. She's going to help us with Grandfather. And this is Caroline, my sister," Darby says, gesturing to the young woman with a severe bob in the same blonde color as her mother's, only slightly shorter.

"So, you're the youngest?" I ask Darby.

"Yes. Gerold, then Barry, then Caroline, and me," she says.

"Accident," Caroline says under her breath.

"Shut up," Darby says back.

"Darby, I don't understand why you're wasting this woman's time. Your grandfather just went for a long walk," Misty says. Her daughter barely looks up from what she is typing. It's as if she's telling a rehearsed story, rather than giving an explanation.

I'm beginning to think all the personality in the Vondale family went directly to Darby. The rest of the family seems to be made up of one-dimensional, privileged bores.

"For three days? Mother, that is completely ridiculous. Yes, it's true he likes to walk the trail around the property, but I've checked over and over, and he's not there. Besides, how many old men do you know who go on three-day walks without telling anyone?" Darby asks.

"Don't get so worked up, it's a waste of energy," Misty says, not looking up from her device.

Family bickering – is it strange that I miss it?

"Can you tell me where your father might have gone, Ms. Vondale?" I interject.

"Father-*in-law*," Misty spells out, looking up. With that, Caroline stands up, surprising me.

"Grandfather is probably off on some quest to find UFOs or Bigfoot or some other insane thing, because that's what crazy people do," Caroline says disapprovingly.

"Shut up, Carol," Darby snaps.

"Don't you dare call me that," Caroline says as she pushes her chair in.

"Okay, well, where would a toilet be around here?" I ask, trying to break the tension.

"Just back down the hall. Take a right, second door," Darby instructs. I'm realizing I do not want this case after all. It's not worth the extra stress. As I walk down the hall, I pass awkward family photos along the walls. Only Darby ever seems to smile in them.

When I take a right turn I bump straight into a man.

A naked man wearing a ski mask.

Out of reflex, I snatch my pepper spray from my coat pocket and point it.

"Who are you?" I ask.

The man lifts the mask and smiles, seemingly without a care that I am pointing the pepper spray at him. Upon closer inspection, I realize he isn't completely naked but wearing barely there swim trunks.

"I'm Troy, who the hell are you?" he asks. Lowering the spray and tucking it back into my coat pocket, my cheeks flush. Troy is fit and his perfect brown skin reflects the hallway light, making him look like the cover of a romance novel. He did not look like a Troy.

"I'm Gray Cooper, PI. I've come to help find Mr. Vondale. Sorry about that, you startled me – the mask – and old habits die hard," I sputter. My cheeks flush even more at the fact I've repeated a phrase Gramma Sugar uses all the time. Speaking to men like I'm ninety-two years old is not going to help my love life. Not that I'm interested in this one.

"I've been known to startle. The old man's fine, probably on a walk," he says.

"That's what everyone keeps telling me. Where do you fit into the family then, Troy?" I ask. He pulls off the ski mask and flutters his eyelashes. Just then Darby rounds the corner.

"Troy, stop distracting Ms. Cooper, she has actual work to do," Darby orders.

"I'm not distracted, and it's Gray." I am suddenly self-conscious. "Why were you wearing that?" I ask, eyeing the ski mask.

"My face gets cold. It was nice to meet you, Gray. Next time we meet I hope you don't point pepper spray at me," Troy says with a wink.

I'm confused.

Why is he in swim trunks in September?

As he leaves the hallway, the scent of birch and black currant lingers.

"Pepper spray? What the—" Darby is wide-eyed.

"He had a ski-mask on, it was inst – I'm sorry," I say.

"That's the most hilarious thing I've heard all day. Troy's my stepdad. God, I hate saying that out loud," Darby says.

"Why isn't he dressed at this time of year?" I ask, unfolding my coat.

"Indoor pool. He never has a shirt on, I think my mom made it a rule." Darby rolls her eyes.

"Alright, then," I say as I pull my trench back on.

"Gray, why haven't you accepted my Coin down payment for the case?" Darby asks. Because I wasn't sure I wanted to take this case at all; because I've never solved even one case; and because I'm afraid if I do take the case, I might love it.

"Listen, I should've been straight with you from the start. The card you found – " I cut myself off, not knowing if I can continue without getting emotional. Darby reaches into her pocket and offers me the card.

My father's card.

Detective Cooper in Garamond typeface, with his number and a tiny golden magnifying glass etched in the corner. Dad thought the cards were "classic and old-timey." I run my thumb over the faded gold foil, and an old pain in my heart clicks into place. It surprises me how deeply I feel this. With Mom, grief feels close to the surface. I looked up at a smiling Darby.

"This is my father's card," I finish. Darby's face falls a bit.

"Oh. So, you aren't a detective?" She is disappointed.

"Well, I do have my license, it's just that this would be my first case," I finally admit. Darby looks relieved and seems to care more if someone is going to help her find her grandfather, than how experienced this person is.

"Alright then, Ms. Coo—Gray, please accept the Coin," Darby says.

"I can't promise you I'll find your grandfather," I say.

"I need someone to try," Darby says. I look into her

desperate eyes and see something familiar. The eyes of a woman who is not accepted by her family. The weird one. And the only person she feels understands her is her grandfather and he is missing. I take out my device and click 'Accept' on the Coin payment.

"Please show me Mr. Vondale's room," I say matter-of-factly.

5

Werner Vondale's room is full of whimsy and dust. There are old Area 51 stickers bordering a small mirror, covered with a thick layer of lint. The bed is neatly tucked, military style, and Darby flounces right onto it. It creaks with age but remains intact.

"Grandfather always let me jump on his bed when I was a kid, and if my mother ever found out I'd be toast," Darby announces. The way Darby talks about her mother's rules sounds youthful, like she hasn't quite grown up yet.

"Sounds like a fun Grandpa," I say, running a finger along the dust on the bedframe.

"He was – is. The cleaning staff is not allowed in here, Grandfather's orders." Darby's smile falls as she remembers what we're doing in his room.

I motion to ask if it's okay to open his drawers, and Darby nods in allowance. Socks, clothing... nothing of note. I go to the closet and begin looking in drawers there, and in cabinets. I search his bathroom, every cubby and drawer. Then I go back into the room and slowly looked around, to see what I might have missed.

Check under the mattress.

"You might want to leave the room for this," I say to Darby. Don't want to scar her for life if I find something gross. She leaves without a word, as I lift the heavy mattress.

Bingo.

I pull out a badge and some paperwork.

"Found something. What's this?" I ask, holding up the badge.

Darby comes around the doorway tentatively.

"Oh, it's his work badge. He works in the Archives Department at the aviation museum," Darby says.

"And these?" I hand Darby the paperwork.

"Life insurance, Werner Vondale," Darby reads, and flips through the pages hurriedly.

"This says he paid a special premium for 'unforeseen circumstances leading to demise,' and it says the beneficiaries are Barold and Gerold Vondale?" Darby's face is incredulous. I reach into my pocket and eat another cinnamon candy.

"Don't say anything to your brothers." I grab the papers from Darby.

"But these were under his mattress, they could have already seen them," Darby says.

"Have they mentioned it yet?" I ask.

"Well, no," Darby says.

"I'm just speculating here, but don't you think if your brothers discovered a pot of money for the untimely demise of your grandfather, they'd mention it? They don't seem like the kind of people to keep such things close to their chest." I am already headed for the front door.

"Where are you going?" Darby asks.

"I'm going to meet a guy about some insurance," I say.

"Wait, I don't understand. He thought my brothers were

the worst, he told me all the time, he didn't understand why Mother let them stay here, and what about Caroline, or *me?*" she asks, her voice cracking.

"That's precisely what I'm about to find out, I'll be in touch," I say as I exit.

6

When I pull into the parking lot, a hanging sign says CLOSED on the door at Mistwell Insurance. As I reverse out of the lot, I let out a sigh. My plan to inquire about the Vondale's policy is not going to happen.

I turn around and head back to my apartment.

Once home, I shuffle up the steps, and the click of the door unlocking feels more like a start gun. Eager, I go directly into research mode. I pull out my phone and look up the Salem Museum of Aviation. There is Werner Vondale's smiling photo with a caption.

Werner Vondale is a retired resident of Salem, MA. Most of his adult life he has served the public as a docent, and as a young man worked for the government in Roswell, NM. He spends his leisure time swimming and devoted to his loving family. If you have him on a tour, make sure you ask him about the time he met an alien.

I scribble down some notes, but when I flip the page in my

notebook, I stop. My own writing stares back at me, in the shape of the fire chief's number.

Ugh.

I've been avoiding thoughts of Mom and the fire, even while I know dealing with it is inevitable.

The big goose egg in her bank account bulges in my mind. Why is it that the most pressing things in life, the things that hold the most potential for disaster, are always the easiest to close off into a corner in the back of one's mind?

Not sure why, but I tear out the paper with the fire chief's number and shove it into the top desk drawer.

I will take care of it later.

I busy myself by learning about the Vondale family until the sun coming in between the blinds fades.

As evening sweeps in, sadness seems to move in with it and I go looking for some comfort in the form of vodka. It's not the healthiest thing to do, I know. But no one is here to stop me or lecture me. Or help me.

I go to the kitchen and peel the plastic off the top of a new bottle. It makes a tiny sigh as I unscrew the cap and take a swig, no glass.

The liquor warms my throat, and I make my way to my favorite cozy chair. I recline and relax. However, each time my eyes close, all I see is flames.

Sitting and sipping, staring bleary-eyed at nothing, I allow my mind to go numb.

I give in.

Surrender to the effort of being in control.

No matter how strong I try to be, how compartmentalized, whenever I'm alone the emotions catch me.

I'm alone a lot these days.

Admittedly, I've been ghosting Lucy and Gramma Sugar.

After all their calls, I haven't returned one. My body feels weak and my mind soft.

I can be a good person later.

Leaning back, I put my head on the chair and look at the ceiling, the room gently spinning. My arm is slung over the side, and I feel my grip on the bottle go slack. I grab for it but it's too late.

The bottle drops.

Smash.

"Shiii…" I slur, as I stand up on the chair, barefoot. I hop to the couch and try to make it over to a clear spot on the floor with grace, avoiding the broken glass.

I find my slippers and clumsily pulled them on before heading to the kitchen for the broom.

A flame flickers in my mind, so I close my eyes tight and try to put it out. I think of my mother, lighting the match, purposely setting the fire.

There is no way.

The thoughts bound forth, even with the vodka edges.

Investigation closed due to suicide.

If my mother were going to do such a thing, burning herself alive seems rife with a kind of terror I could not attribute to my glamorous do-gooder mother. Sweeping up the glass, I shuffle it into the dustpan when I hear a familiar voice.

"I know what you're thinking, Gray Meliodas," Mom says as she reclines on the same sofa I had just tramped across.

I startle at the sight of her, dropping the broom.

I'm definitely losing my mind.

"Mom, don't scare me like that," I say.

"Scare you like what darling…a ghost?" Mom laughs. How is this funny?

"What am I thinking?" I hug myself and sit in the chair.

"Dear?" Mom asks.

"You said you know what I'm thinking, so tell me what *am I* thinking?" I am serious but the words come out slower than expected. The alcohol has my tongue.

"Gray, I didn't kill myself."

Thank god.

"I know you didn't. Jesus, Mom, if you really wanted to, you would have found some environmentally sound way," I say knowingly. It's funny, but I still feel confused.

"But are you real?" Tears gathering at the corners of my eyes.

"Oh, darling. Yes. It's me, but I'm in another realm."

"But I'm not seeing things or hearing voices? Like your voice? Because I feel like this is a hallucination."

"No, I'm not a hallucination."

"And you didn't kill yourself?"

"No, but I did set the fire," Mom says, with mischief in her lifted eyebrows.

"You what?" I am trying hard to concentrate but realize that keeping my eyes open is a task my overloaded brain can barely accomplish.

It's a confusing thing having your deceased parent visit so soon after their passing. I was devastated learning of my mother's death. My mother was the steady guiding force in my life. She was healthy and vital and part of me always felt that she could defy mortality and live forever.

Her death was an utter shock.

While I feel lucky and grateful to see the apparition of my mother, it doesn't feel quite as satisfying as one might imagine. How can I grieve someone who is still sort of here?

I'm unsettled by the questions my visits with Mom pose, but even more so by the questions I can't stop asking of myself. What could this mean about me, am I seeing a ghost? Am I losing my mind? Was the shock of Mom's death too much for me, and now I've created this whole ghost thing for comfort?

There is a knock at the door.

Who could be visiting this late? Did a neighbor hear the bottle break?

Shining stars float beneath my lids.

Wake up.

Answer the door.

When I get there, I will my hand to the doorknob. When I finally manage to open the door, nothing greets me but the brisk night.

Weird.

But before I shut it, I see a brown box sitting on the stoop. Staring out to the street, I give one last look around for a delivery vehicle, but the night is quiet.

Weirder.

I slam and lock the door, package in hand, and I find myself quite sober.

"Mom, just a delivery," I announce, walking back into the living room.

And again, my mother is gone.

"Why do you leave before we discuss anything?" I call out to the empty room. Is she a ghost or a figment of my imagination? I can't be one hundred percent sure.

But part of me believed her when she said she was real.

I miss her.

My heart breaks every time I hear the unforgettable honey of her voice.

I head to the kitchen for scissors and set to opening the unmarked box. I take a breath before pulling the flaps open. I've seen movies where opening a mysterious box is not the best idea. It could be something awful...or it could be cinnamon candy.

I pull the flaps up and remove the crumpled paper on top. Inside there is a thick book.

The Paranormal and Their Search for Meaning.

Thumbing through the finely printed pages, my head begins to spin. Who sent me a book? It seems like something my father would have read.

My spiraling thoughts get the better of me. Paranormal. I mean we live in Salem, Massachusetts, it's all around us. All those books about witches and aliens and werewolves. Dad's business was paranormal, he investigated supernatural cases.

Mom is paranormal. I think she's a ghost, and Dad would have believed it. Without question. And now something inside me says I believe it too.

Time for bed.

I prop the book on my nightstand, knowing there is no way I can read right now.

Later.

I clean up, click off all the lights, put the broom away, and go to bed.

7

Late the next morning, I arrive at Mistwell clutching the packet of insurance papers from Werner Vondale's room. I shut the door of Hero hard and pat it as if to say, "good girl."

The glass door greets me with a closed sign.

Not again.

This time I hear music coming from inside, so I knock and peer in through the window glass like a nosey neighbor. There on the front counter, I can see the same worn gray leather jacket I'd noticed on Joe's chair the last time I was here.

He's here.

Well, Joe, I have some things to discuss with you.

I knock again with force. This time the door pushes in a bit, and although the closed sign is up... I mean, the door is unlocked. The open door is an invitation, so I open it.

"Mr. Nebraska?" I call out. No hoodied assistant. Music blares from Joe's office and so I make my way past the front desk.

I only push on the office door gently, and it too opens into the dark. The Beatles', *Don't Let Me Down* blares from the lit bathroom on the left.

"Mr. Nebraska, I wanted to ask you about something – " I begin, but then freeze, because just at that moment Joe exits the bathroom.

I didn't realize how I might appear to him – an unfamiliar silhouette standing in his office when they are closed.

It's dark, and Joe instantly grabs a crystal Mistwell paperweight from the shelf in front of him and lobs it at the shadowy figure – being me.

I duck.

The paperweight explodes against the wall near my head, just as I find the light switch.

"Stop!" I hold out my hands toward him. Joe, wearing just a towel on his taut frame, hair slicked back, freezes. We both stand still for what seems like an eternity.

My hand holding the papers is shaking as I make a surrender gesture with the other, and Joe stands dripping from the shower. His body is more muscular than I'd have guessed. The towel is tucked along his tight waistline.

Our eyes meet, and his soften when he recognizes that it's me. He bends forward and starts laughing hysterically.

"I'm sorry to interrupt," I say quickly. I can't help but smile too.

"Ms. Cooper. I'm sorry I threw that thing at you, are you okay?" he asks.

"Yes, I'm fine. Um...yes, I needed to ask you about something," I stutter. Running into scantily clad men by surprise is becoming a dangerous habit.

"Good thing I have terrible aim. Wasn't the closed sign up?" he asks, clutching the waist of his towel, suddenly self-conscious.

"Yes, sign is up, but the door is unlocked, so I –" I cut

myself off. Of course, I shouldn't have come in when the sign said CLOSED. That's me, being presumptuous again.

"Well, let me throw on some clothes and we can discuss?" he offers, still smiling.

"Okay, sure." I stumble as I back out of the office, shuffle through the broken glass, and shut the door.

My ears are hot, and my pulse begins thudding in my neck.

Well, sure we can discuss the Vondale case if I don't die of embarrassment first. I start rubbing the bridge of my nose. This is not how I planned for things to go.

My whole dynamic with Joe Nebraska has just exploded like the paperweight against the wall.

I choose to wait for Joe in Hero, because it is impossible for me to stay in that office one more moment. Rolling the cornered edges of Werner Vondale's insurance papers, over and over again, I try to shake my mind from seeing Joe in that towel.

Joe taps on my window, and I gasp. He gives a wave, and I unlock the door to get out, since unrolling the window isn't an easy task. As I open my door, Joe opens the passenger side door and sits down beside me.

Okay, we are sitting in the car.

I shut the door.

"Nice car," he says. The scent of clean pine and shaving cream fills the air. Still trying not to notice how the leather jacket fits precisely over his shoulders, I tug the waistbelt of my trench coat tighter.

"Thanks, I call her Hero. Because she saved me once."

"Now that sounds like a story I want to hear," he says over-enthusiastically.

"Maybe some other time. For now, I need some help, and I thought —"

"You thought, hey, I'll find that guy I threatened and break into his office to ask him for help," he says lightly.

My hands grip the steering wheel.

"Mr. Nebraska, you can get out now." I don't have time for passive-aggressive banter. And this whole situation is so uncomfortable.

I'm done.

"It's Joe, and I'm just trying to understand where you're coming from. You are one confusing lady," he says. I place my fingers on the sides of my face, as though it will fix everything, but it never does.

Maybe I can explain?

"I'm sorry about before, and now. There is a lot going on, and I just made things worse by taking on my first case, which I have no business doing while tying up my mother's affairs, and now my father's too," I unload.

"Your father has passed too? I'm so sorry to hear," Joe says with genuine concern.

"Yes, he was declared dead ten years ago, killed on a job. I'm sorry, but I really don't want to talk about it," I say, squeezing the pressure point between my thumb and index finger, a habit my mother taught me.

"So, what's this case you have?" he asks, noticing my discomfort. I hand him the papers with the overly curled corners, and I'm grateful for the subject change.

"Werner Vondale. He left the house without any belongings two nights ago after dinner. According to his granddaughter Darby, he was in his right mind and never said anything about leaving. I was wondering if you find these papers to be legit, because his life insurance policy left everything to two grandsons he could barely stand. And Darby was particularly close to him, but he left her nothing."

Joe looks more invested than I expected, as he fingers through the paperwork.

"Okay, so...three things – one, the paperwork looks legit. Two, there could be a will with other stipulations. And three, I know the Vondales so I probably shouldn't get involved," he says.

"You know them? Tell me everything." I couldn't help but beam at my luck, finding someone who could truly help my case. Joe reaches for the door handle and starts to exit Hero.

"Not today, Ms. Cooper, sorry."

What?

"You can't leave me hanging like that," I say, frustrated.

"I'm sorry, I've got an appointment and have to go. Why don't we meet for a drink, maybe tomorrow evening. We can talk then," he says.

Crap.

Drinks?

I'm afraid where this road will lead, Joe and I having a drink, commiserating and collaborating. In the past, I've been burned by charming men in leather jackets. He seems sincere, and a youthful hope exudes from his face. I can make this strictly about business.

I've been quiet too long.

"Yes, okay, but only to discuss the Vondales' and my mother's case. A professional meeting," I say, and he smiles.

"I promise not to wear my towel," Joe says as he exits Hero.

"Where?" I call after him.

"The Uncanny, 8p.m.?" he asks, leaning his arm on the car roof, with the door still open. Why does he have to be like this? He makes everything feel like a movie.

"Alright," I confirm.

The Uncanny. Of course he'd pick the diviest dive bar in

Salem. He shuts the door to the car, and I watch him as he goes back inside Mistwell.

"Well, that one's not too shabby on the eyes," Mom says from the passenger seat.

"Mother," I gasp, "stop sneaking up on me like that."

My nervous system refuses to get used to this. This time, though, I try on the possibility that she's a ghost.

"Well, darling, sneaking is kind of inevitable," Mom says matter-of-factly.

8

"Mom, I have so many things I want to talk to you about, can you please stay longer this time?" I say to preface this new appearance of my mother.

"I don't quite have control over how long I'm here. Apparently, I'm supposed to be tending to unfinished business," Mom says.

And I believe her. She's really back. I'm not sure how, but she is.

"Tell me what happened? You said you set the fire, and Joe Nebraska has a letter that looks like a suicide note – in your handwriting. I'm trying to deal with you being gone, but you're still sort of here. Why did you set the fire?" I ask, hoping that she will stay long enough to tell me something important. Or maybe just stay longer, because I miss her.

"I was trying to get in touch with your father," Mom says delicately.

"Dad? Mom we both know he's dead." I'm even more confused than I was before. If my father is alive somewhere, why would they tell us he was dead? How could Mom move on with George? Why did they give Dad a gravestone? It just doesn't make sense.

I must focus, because my questions are growing new questions, and I know we are short on time.

"Your father is not dead, Gray," she says. My heart starts racing. I literally don't think I can take another shock. Even though adrenaline courses through me, the thought that I might not in fact be an orphan warms the formerly cold places inside me.

"What do you mean 'not dead'? How could you let me believe he was dead this whole time?" I say, anger rising in my throat. Glancing out the window, I want to make sure Joe doesn't see me talking to myself.

"Well, I didn't exactly say he was alive, either," she says.

Now I'm feeling full fury; this game of this or that with the facts has to stop.

"Where is Dad?" I can't hold back.

"Darling, don't be so demanding, it's unbecoming. Your father is trapped somewhere. He is not dead, although I'm sure he feels like he is. It's all in the contract, but it's very complicated and I cannot tell you more, or you will be in danger," Mom says.

Tears of anger streak down my face. What contract? What kind of danger?

"I don't care about being in danger. Tell me – I want to help you and Dad, please." I'm begging, because danger is relative. My sanity is in danger due to the lack of information I have about the people I love the most.

"Well, there is one thing you could do," Mom says, seeing how pained I am.

"Name it."

"Gray, I need you to drop the Vondale case," Mom says quietly. Her ghostly flickers are beginning to fade.

"How do you even know about the case?" I ask. This is just great; my mother comes and wants me to drop the one thing I feel good about.

"Gray, I don't know how they know about it, but trust me – if they know it's for a reason. Please – drop the case," Mom says. She reaches out to pat me on the shoulder, only her hand mists right through it.

I look at her, sad and contrite. *Who are 'they' anyway?*

"No," I say simply.

Mom looks at me with concern in her brow. The wispy vapors of her form fade away, and I lose my mother for the fourth time.

My mind is swimming.

There is no way to process it all right now. I don't trust myself.

But one thing I *do* trust is that I know how to investigate. Finding answers is something I can focus on.

Because answers are solid. Facts are solid.

I'll treat my mom and dad as separate cases, not unlike the Vondale case. Three cases – Vondale, Mom and Dad. Not going to focus on the fact that I have yet to solve even one.

Vondale is my priority since Werner Vondale is likely still alive and can be found. Next, I'll look for my father, because although it is highly unlikely, if he too is still alive I must try and find him. Finally, I will determine how my mother died in a fire that she herself admitted to setting and prove it was not a suicide.

I can do this; I can do all of it.

Easy.

9

Your father is trapped somewhere. He is not dead, although I'm sure he feels like he is. It's all in the contract. This is all I can think of since my mother spoke those words yesterday. How is he trapped somewhere, and what contract is she referring to?

I've been picking through files all day in my father's office searching for this contract. Even though my grand plan was to attack the Vondale case first, I can't get my dad out of my mind.

This is exactly why I don't trust myself.

As soon as I find the contract, it will explain everything, and then I'll get to Vondale.

This would have been a much easier task if Woody Cooper had kept a tidy and organized office, but instead it is packed with paperwork and evidence files that have no rhyme or reason I can detect. I'm surrounded by my father's life's work, and if it were possible for clutter to give me a hug, this is exactly how it would feel.

When I look up at the clock, it's 7:46 p.m., and I feel like I need to stop and take a break. Standing to stretch my stiff legs,

I lean on the desk and look out the window. A black square of darkness. On the weathered windowsill I spot papers folded and tucked into the gap of the window jam.

Curious.

I pull the papers out and sit on the sill to read.

CERTIFICATE OF TERMINATION OF CONTRACT,
BETWEEN WOODMAN COOPER AND THE UNITED
STATES TERMS OF INDEPENDENT CONTRACT
[REDACTED]
REASON FOR TERMINATION: DEATH OF
WOODMAN COOPER

It all feels so final.

There isn't room between the large block letters to think anything except for exactly what they confirm – that Woodman Cooper had indeed died. That feels real and right, no matter what my mom told me.

The truth is, that Mom didn't tell me much at all. Could this be the contract my mother was talking about? Underneath the termination paper is something even more final, a copy of my father's death certificate.

Death Certificate of Woodman Cooper
Cause of Death: Presumption of death due to abandonment of duty and family

Presumption? And that word.

Abandonment.

It was so far out of character that Woody Cooper, a quirky PI who loved his family, would just abruptly leave and not make contact for a decade.

It is unfathomable.

And painful.

I know in my heart that he has to be, he *must* be dead.

Just then I hear a loud *thump* coming from the bathroom. I grab my pepper spray and make my way over to the bathroom.

"Is someone there?" I ask the air.

No one answers.

Holding up the pepper spray in my right hand, I slowly open the bathroom door and flick on the light with my left. I'm at the ready. The bathroom is empty, but I stare at the door on the other wall.

The office next door shares a bathroom door.

I try the handle, but it is locked as usual. The sound was probably someone in the neighboring office.

Before Woody's time, they must have sold or rented out both offices as one, but ever since Dad purchased his office space, the door has been locked. He figured he got the good end of the deal, because whoever rents the other space has to use the community bathroom in the hallway.

I remember Dad planned to have the door removed and the wall filled in, but like many things, he never got around to actually doing it.

Putting my ear to the door like I'm in some old-fashioned movie, I hope to hear something – maybe Mom? But nothing stirs.

For the first time since I've revisited the office, I look around the bathroom, and it's clear it has not been cleaned in years. The film in the sink has turned orange, and dust on the back of the toilet is thick.

Gross.

Note to self – bring cleaning supplies next time.

I pick through the dusty reading material collected in the basket on the small countertop. *A Guide for Fit Survival*, *The Witches Almanac*, and *A Primer on Werewolves*.

That was Woody, always enthralled by notions of the occult. He claimed to have a gift for helping those with supernatural problems, and I was absolutely mortified by him.

Growing up, I tried to keep my friends from finding out what he did for a living. Usually, I could get away with saying he was a PI, but once people found out what kind of PI, well, that was an invitation to the social pariah club.

I had wanted so desperately for my father to do something pragmatic, like be a software engineer like Penny's dad, or a stay-at-home father like Louis's. But no, Woody Cooper was a PI, investigating crimes of the bizarre and the supernatural.

My mother, Madeline, was the practical parent and tried to bridge the gap, being the lover of nature and order. Mom told me there wasn't a divide between the natural and the supernatural; there was room for both.

Woody was less understanding of my embarrassment, and often shooed me away, telling me to "just wait until you're older. Your brain doesn't fully form until age twenty-six. Then come and see me."

By the time I turned twenty-six, he was gone, and he hadn't shared any deep secrets about the world or explained his affinity with the paranormal. I had to go on explaining it to myself, my own way. The natural world is the truth, the trees and the Earth and the seasons. The rest is just entertainment.

Maybe I'm more Mom than Dad. But if Mom is a ghost, what does that make *me*?

I tuck the survival book under my arm and turn off the light in the bathroom.

I sit on a heavy box and start to read through, *A Guide for Fit Survival*, noticing my father's notes in the margins.

READING THE WEATHER

In this chapter, Woody had written, "Storm: wear glasses, chocolate on hand and thank Tempestates." Wonder what Tempestates means? I continue flipping through the book, and what I find next, causes me to inhale deeply.

SURVIVING DEATH

Woody has left so many notes in the margins, I'm sure there will be something here to help me understand what happened to him.

My phone rings.

It's Joe Nebraska.

Shoot!

I'm supposed to meet him at the The Uncanny at 8:00 p.m.

"This is Gray," I answer. My stomach is a pit.

"Gray, just wanted to let you know I'm running a bit behind tonight. Can we meet at 8:30?" Joe asks.

I'm not sure what to say, because I'm relieved but also distracted. It feels like I'm on the brink of discovering something important about my father's disappearance, but on the other hand, Joe is going to help me with the Vondale case.

I can either keep reading and digging through files, or go investigate the actual case I'm being paid for…

"No problem," I say.

"Great, see you then," he says, and hangs up.

I fold up my father's papers and jam them along with the book into my square leather satchel. Throwing on my trench coat, I grab a candy from the tin in my pocket and chew it as I lock up my father's office.

10

The Uncanny is a bar that I have passed by many times, but never actually entered. It's frequented by locals, biker gangs, and those who don't mind that the tap is mostly held together with duct tape, a fun fact my friend Lucy told me once. Shit, I really need to call her.

Tonight, there's a line outside, mostly college kids. Tall boys—men wearing athleisure and poufy hairdos. A girl wearing a lot of necklaces twirls her hair nervously and looks around for someone. This is unexpected: a line to drink warm beer from a duct-taped tap. I approach the bouncer by the door.

"Why there's a line tonight?" I ask.

"Trivia night," says the bouncer who looks at me warmly, then he adds, "You can go in though." I looked back at the short line of young men, figured this is some sort of chivalry, and walk toward the door. The bouncer holds his hand up.

"Wait," he says. His pudgy face is plain.

"I thought you said I could go in?" I'm confused.

"ID," he says with a smile.

This could have been charming, but my patience is

waning. I bungle the wallet out of my satchel, and it drops to the ground. As I bend over, the rowdy college kids cheer. I roll my eyes, and show him my ID. He looks at it, smiles, and waves his hand toward the door as if I'm about to enter Oz.

Like many bars in Salem, there's a witchy theme to the place. Cast-iron silhouettes of witches hang on the walls and little cauldron's hold tea lights on the tables in the booths. It smells like stale popcorn and skunky beer. There are orange twinkle lights hanging along the six booths, which are packed with twentysomethings.

There's a DJ with his laptop precariously balanced on an apple crate standing upright on a folding tray in the corner. His headphones are flickering with neon lights.

Behind him, on the last stool at the bar and farthest from the door, Joe sits in his leather jacket.

The second I spot him, my cheeks flush. His jacket hugs him just right. The light from the bar hits his cheekbones, and he's a classic movie star.

Stop.

I hate when my body reacts without permission. Reaching into my coat pocket, I grab candy to soothe my nerves.

Joe stands as we make eye contact, and he beckons me over.

"I ordered you a beer," he says loudly, so I can hear him over the EDM pumping from the speakers. The gesture is kind, but there was no way I'm drinking that.

I sit down next to him.

"I appreciate it, but I'm a vodka kind of gal," I say, pushing my beer next to his.

"Alright. Hey Rooster, can you get the lady a vodka?" he says.

"Ice," I add.

"On ice," he says, as Rooster comes over with his long hair

and one arm. He's wearing a black skull bandana and painted blue fingernails.

"I gotchoo" he says, as he scoops a glass into the ice chest, then tosses the vodka bottle into the air with a flip and places the drink in front of me.

"Impressive." I smile and clap – I can't help it. Rooster winks at me as he moves down the bar.

"Thanks for being flexible," Joe says, wincing as he takes a sip of his beer. I look around at the boisterous folks filling almost every seat. There is a carefree spirit in them that I envy.

I take a deep breath.

"This place is not what I expected," I say, not clueing him in on the fact that I'd nearly forgotten our meeting all together.

"Yeah, I forgot about trivia night. It's usually not like this," he says, as he takes off his jacket. The air is scented with Joe's spicy aftershave. Each move he makes is more irresistible than the last. Feeling warm, I pull off my trench, and take out a notebook from my bag.

"Is this going to be an interview?" he jokes.

"You were going to tell me about the Vondale's," I say, feeling sheepish about being all business, when I do really want to be social.

Be free. Like all the kids around me.

"Yes, so – what do you want to know?"

"First off, how do you know them?" I ask. Joe is quiet for a long minute and picks at the worn rope bracelet on his wrist.

"I was doing some consulting work for Caroline." Joe takes another swig of his beer. Darby's pretty and cold older sister. They dated; I can tell by his body language. Biting his lip, hands clenched — means it didn't end well. Not the type I'd guess he'd be into, but I suppose opposites do attract.

"And did you meet the grandfather, Mr. Vondale?" I ask.

"Oh yeah, he's a cool old cat. Used to work for the government, something top secret, when he lived in Nevada," Joe says. Nevada. Area 51. I can't help but think – maybe I'm more like Dad than I thought.

"How long ago?" I ask.

"A long time ago, back in his twenties, I think. They moved to Massachusetts to start a family," he says.

"They have extended family here?" I ask, wondering why Massachusetts specifically.

"Not sure. I think they liked the access to universities and museums. Old Man Vondale works at a museum, he's really into history. I think some of the things he learned while working for the government bled into his own personal interests."

"Like aliens?" I ask, thinking back to the Area 51 stickers on Werner Vondale's mirror.

"Yeah, he definitely had a thing about aliens," Joe says. So did my father.

"What do you think?" I laugh.

"About aliens? I don't know. The fact that humans exist at all is so remote, can't rule it out," he says.

That's an open answer. I like that Joe doesn't judge him, but we can talk about aliens another time. Right now, I need to know about the more earthly subject of life insurance and heirs.

"Was he close with his grandchildren? Particularly the boys?" I focus back on the case.

"Honestly, they're both egomaniacal jerks, and I don't think that was lost on Vondale," he says. My phone buzzes. The screen lights up with a message from Darby.

"Sorry, I should take this," I say.

Gray – the museum wants me to collect grandfather's belongings. Can you meet me at my house, and we'll go together? They open at 10am.

I wonder why Darby doesn't want to meet at the museum but figure we could talk about the case on the way.

Sure, Darby. Pick you up at 9:45am.

I look back at Joe, who is more patient with me than I am with myself.

"Speak of the devil, that was Darby. I'm meeting up with her in the morning." I take a sip of my drink. "So, back to the brothers, I got the jerk vibe too, but why would Vondale leave them his money?" I ask, pushing my hair behind my ear.

"Couldn't tell you," he says, taking a swig of his beer. More people crowd into The Uncanny, and my neck burns with the sensation of someone watching me. I glance around the room but see no one obvious.

Weird.

The DJ suddenly stops playing music and instead announces over the microphone, "Welcome to trivia night at Uncanny!"

The crowd thunders applause.

"It might be a bit loud for this." I point at my notebook.

The DJ yells, "To get us started, we'll have a conversation warmup." The crowd cheers.

"So, answer this question within your groups: What is the worst thing that has ever happened to you at work? Jessa is going to go around with the microphone, and you can pick your table's best response. Again, what is the worst thing that has ever happened to you at work? This is a juicy one, folks," he says.

I look at Joe, smiling.

"Well, Joe, what is the worst thing that has ever happened to *you* at work?" I joke.

But Joe has lost the calm, cool demeanor he always has. His face is drained of color, and he pulls on his jacket.

"I think you're right. Let's get outta here. Too loud," he

says. Joe flashes his phone at the QR on the counter to pay and heads directly for the door.

I grab my coat to follow him. Thinking it was a harmless question, now I'm more curious than ever for him to answer it.

Outside in the quiet night air, the murmurs from the bar feel far away, and my eyes become glossy from the cold. Joe shivers.

"Once, I split my pants when tying my shoe, when I was a nursing home aide," I confide. Joe's face is too serious to process the joke.

"Oh, funny," he says, without an inkling of sarcasm or humor.

"Well – " I start.

"I should get going," Joe says. The night air is cold, I hug myself in a brief tremble.

"Wow, already?" I straighten. I've touched a nerve. Well, technically the DJ did with his question, but my curiosity is not helping.

"If there are any more questions I can answer, please call or text. Have a lovely night, Gray Cooper."

Joe leans in for a half- hug, and taps my shoulder. Something is definitely taking residence in his head. I stand here accepting this new energy.

Then he turns and leaves into the night.

I'm left with more questions.

11

Wake up.

It's early. Too early.

I rub my eyes and stumble toward the bathroom, realizing staying awake nearly twenty-four hours isn't ideal.

Last night after my meetup with Joe I couldn't focus on the Vondales, because it I could only think of Joe. When I think of Joe, I can't think about anything else.

And I saw it there on the nightstand, the book. *The Paranormal and Their Search for Meaning*, an 800-page tome I ended up completing just as the sun was rising. Not sure if I learned anything specifically applicable to my parents, but I'm glad I read it all the same.

Feeling slightly more human after my shower, I prepare to meet with Darby. I fill two travel mugs with coffee, because I can tell it's going to be one of those days.

I pull the pile of paperwork and notebook off the table where I left it, and I realize I'm going to need a more organized way to carry my work. Lucy, my best friend, told me throughout PI school that I needed a briefcase. But I find briefcases to be too cumbersome and dated.

Thinking of Lucy makes my chest twinge in regret. I really must call her.

It's me. My fault.

As I make my way out to Hero, I notice the long list of missed calls on my phone.

Later, Gray.

As I drive to the Vondales', I have that feeling again. The feeling of being followed. Yet, every time I look in my mirrors, I don't see anything or anyone. Maybe it's Mom.

Pulling Hero into the driveway, my eye twitches. I take a deep breath, hoping to breathe out the pressure I feel building behind my face.

The house has somehow grown more ornate than the first time I was here. The entryway hosts the scent of freshly polished mahogany. Phyllis, a housekeeper asks to take my coat, and I oblige. I grab some cinnamon candies from the pocket before handing the trench over to her. Darby leads me into an office along the hallway, the same hallway where I'd met her barely dressed stepfather. Luckily, he is nowhere in sight today.

Once inside the office, Darby sits down on the couch.

"Tell me what you've found?"

"I'm afraid I have some bad news about the life insurance," I started. "It looks like the benefactors of your grandfather's inheritance really are your brothers."

"I don't understand." Darby is crestfallen.

"I'd like to visit the museum and see if I can find out anything from his coworkers, maybe they have a theory on what happened to him," I say. Darby wipes away an errant tear.

"They won't know anything, Grandfather always called them obtuse," Darby says.

"Note taken, but you never know. I am curious about Mr. Vondale's interest in aliens?" I ask. I'm not sure what kind of reaction I expected to get from this question, but Darby sits up straight, her whole energy ignited.

"Well, he had an *encounter* when he was young, and he always told people it was a happy, fun experience. But it wasn't entirely. He didn't tell anyone the truth about it. Except me. He said he could trust me, because I was the mature one in the family," she says proudly.

"Tell me about this encounter."

"Okay, well, he said when he was about sixteen, he saw a real alien in the woods, and that they fought, because he was afraid. But then they became friends. The alien left a big impression on him, and he's been obsessed with them ever since. I think he dreamed that his friend would visit again," Darby said.

"Did he say that?" I ask.

"No, but when he told me he got teary, and I could tell there was a lot more to the story," Darby says. Her face reflects that sadness, the chance of her hearing the full story from him seems a bit less likely now, with him missing.

"Darby, did your grandfather have any mental health issues?"

"No. He's not crazy. At all. He really did meet an alien," she says. And I know that look in Darby's eyes, that determined protection of the supernatural.

It reminds me of Dad, a steadfast believer in all things occult. After reading the book about the supernatural, I'll admit it seems much more plausible. The book did a great job of reminding me of all the little miracles we consider normal in the everyday world.

When I was young, I'd listen to Dad on his client calls, and I swore they were always talking about some sort of alien, werewolf, or mystical creature, though my mother would disagree and tell me I was misinterpreting. Then she'd admonish me for eavesdropping.

Speaking of my mother, she herself is a ghost these days.

"I believe you," I say to Darby finally as she gets up.

I follow her down the long hallway, the sound of Misty Vondale's voice is unmistakable.

"Darby, dear."

"Yes, mother," Darby responds to the disembodied voice.

"We're in the East Parlor, please do come and invite Ms. Cooper as well," she calls in a voice that is both authoritative and false at the same time.

Darby looks at me with I-don't-know eyes. I nod in assurance. She leads me to a rounded door. The knob is a gold boar's head.

Inside, I am surprised to find the entire Vondale crew assembled. Barry is pacing, and Gerald stands akimbo by the fireplace. Misty sits on a large red leather couch, flanked by Caroline and Troy.

"What's all this?" Darby asks.

Feels like some sort of intervention. I swallow my discomfort.

"Darby, Ms. Cooper, we'd like to speak to you about this ridiculous focus on my father-in-law. We as a family, have decided the case is over," Misty declares.

"You can't. Not until we find Grandfather," Darby says.

"That's the thing, dear. Ms. Cooper here hasn't shown us she can find out anything about where he's run off to," Misty says.

I'll admit that stings.

"Mrs. Vondale, I assure y –" I begin.

"No. Gray has shown more interest in finding him than any of you have. I am using my own trust money to pay her, so you have no say in it," Darby says.

"Listen, Mrs. Vondale, I understand that all of you are quite worried about Mr. Vondale. Darby and I were just about to visit the museum and speak to his coworkers, and I want you to know that this case is my number one priority," I lie, feeling defensive.

"It's a waste of money," Caroline chimes in.

"That's for me to decide," Darby snips.

Suddenly, the meeting is interrupted by Phyllis.

"I'm sorry, he insisted," Phyllis says. Behind her stands a wiry man with long straggly hair. He makes eye contact with me and it sends a shiver up my neck.

"You Gray Cooper?" he asks like he already knows.

I give him the side eye.

"Yeah," I say, unsure I want to admit it.

"You've been served," he says, handing me documents. I stand up straight in surprise.

"Wait, have you been following me?" I say, recognizing the uneasy feeling I've had the last few days.

He raises his hands.

"Part of the job," he says, and turns to leave.

I quickly scan the first page of the document.

It is an announcement of the settlement of Woodman Cooper's estate and says that I should call immediately to settle and make a payment of $100,000 or the office and its contents will go to auction. I don't have that kind of money lying around. I look up from the papers at the Vondale family, humiliated and angry.

"I'm sorry, Darby, I've got to go," I say.

"See? She doesn't care about Grandfather. You might as well flush your trust down the sink," Barry says.

"Toilet," Gerald adds.

Darby looks at me wide-eyed. I'm a terrible person. Her brothers are brats, idiotic brats, but they are right, I am a waste of money. All I ever had to offer her was my empathy. She needs hard facts. How can I help her and my own family? I don't know, but I'll find some way.

"Darby, I'm going to the museum. But I must take care of something first," I say.

I rush out to the entryway and collect my coat. Darby follows but keeps her distance. With the summons in one hand, I grab my phone with the other and my thumb hovers over the name *Mom* in my contact list. I can't bring myself to erase my mother from my phone yet. Even if I can't call her anymore.

It's proof that she was alive.

Who am I supposed to call now? When I need support, both practical and emotional? There are only three people listed on my go-to list – Mom, Lucy, and Gramma Sugar. The saddest, truest fact is that I can't call any of them.

With the phone call left undone, I can go straight to the museum.

I look up to find Darby watching me with pity in her eyes.

"Don't do that," I snap, and open the door to leave. There is no way I can allow a client to pity me, I am not her problem. I was hired to *solve* her problem.

"Do you still want to come with me?" I ask.

"No," Darby says. She turns away and goes down the hall.

I get it. I'll make it up to her.

"I'm sorry, I'll call you," I say to her back.

Outside, the fresh air dries the sweat that had beaded on my upper lip.

I look down at the papers and read *Must Call Immediately to Settle*.

Focus, Gray, focus.

One thing at a time.

All I can do right now is get to the museum and find out more about Werner Vondale and his exploits with aliens. I'll figure out what to do about the settlement afterward.

12

Salem is a city full of museums for all of its historical moments: the birthplace of Nathaniel Hawthorne, a maritime historical site, and perhaps most famously, the Salem witch trials. I pull into the parking lot for The Salem Museum of Aviation, where Werner Vondale spent his last three decades.

I signed in on the guest clipboard at the front and waited to be taken on a private tour. Scrolling on my phone mindlessly, I try to distract myself from the full-tilt emotional rollercoaster I've been on for weeks.

"Hi, I'm Dan. Is anybody ready to see some planes and engines?" a man asks, with too much enthusiasm. I glance over at Dan.

He's shorter than me, blond spikey hair, wearing brown plastic grandma frames and a tucked in black tee shirt that says, *Nacho Average Aircraft Lover*, with a photo of a tortilla chip piloting a plane.

This is going to be something.

"I saaaiiiid, is anybody ready to –" he sings.

"Actually, I'm curious about UFOs," I cut him off.

"Oh, I see," he says, smiling. "You must mean the exhibit on loan from the National Air Force Museum with the UFO artifacts, from the Advanced Aviation Threat Identification Program. Right this way!"

How does Dan have so much energy?

"This program started in 2007 but was defunded by the Pentagon in 2012. The items in the exhibit have been touring ever since. It's a pity our docent Werner isn't here today because this is right up his alley," he says.

"Is he home sick?" I ask, gauging Dan's reaction.

"Oh, no. He hasn't been here all week. Not sure why," he says. I'm not sure if it's his personality or the way he tucks in his teeshirt, but I decide to take a chance on Dan.

"Dan, can I tell you something top secret?" I say conspiratorially.

He pauses.

Then leans closer.

"You can," he whispers.

"I have it on good authority that Werner Vondale might be on a special visit." and I look up for effect. Dan looks up too.

"I knew it. Are you government?" he whispers.

"Top secret," I say.

"Knew. It. The moment I saw your trench coat. Who wears a real trench coat in Salem, you know?" Dan is giddy.

"Oh, I know," I say.

"What can I do for you?" he asks.

"I need to get into Werner's locker. You think you can handle that?" I ask. He takes a deep breath, considering. This will be difficult for Dan, asking him to break the rules. But I can see the rebel beneath the glasses.

"That is completely against all museum policies," he says, and turns around and waves me on to follow him.

He looks both ways, and we pass through a gray unmarked

door, which leads past a break room and down a short hallway to a small row of green lockers.

"What's your name?" he stops to ask.

"I can't tell you that," I say apologetically.

"Oh, right," he says knowingly. He tries to open locker number four, but it's locked. Shoot.

"Don't move. If anyone asks, say you're here to fix the vending machine. I'll be right back," he says as he runs back down the hallway.

I immediately take out my locksmith set and open locker number four.

It is Werner Vondale's. Inside are more stickers like the ones on his mirror at home. The locker door holds a pulp poster from a sci-fi quarterly of a nude woman being held by an alien whose tentacles cover just the right spots on her body. There's a thermos, an airplane keychain, a worn certificate for Employee of the Month, an old can of cashews, and a stack of papers.

I shuffle through the papers quickly, hoping to finish my search before anyone catches me.

There are several Area 51 brochures, and what catches my eye is how recent they are, and not from the time Mr. Vondale had originally worked there. They are from this year. There is a folded-up map, and a printout of train routes leaving from Boston to Nevada.

Who prints out maps anymore? Old dudes.

Looks like Mr. Vondale was planning a trip. I take photos of the train schedule and map and place them back inside the locker.

I bet when I research those train lines, I'll find that Werner Vondale was on one of them. He likely didn't want to clue in his judgy family that he wanted to take one more excursion to his old stomping grounds. It would've been easier on Darby if he had clued her in on it. But maybe he knew she'd want to go with him, and he needed a solo trip. Whatever the reason, I'm willing to bet that I can prove Werner Vondale went to Nevada. And when I do, case closed.

As I slam the locker closed, a tired woman with long blue nails stands looking at me.

"Uh, I came to fix the vending machine," I say. She shrugs.

I make a quick exit to the museum entrance.

13

I unlace my shoes and toss them to the floor.

Afternoon is turning into evening and I'm glad to be home. I fill a mug with vodka, just enough to warm me. As I land back on the couch, I stare at the pile of paperwork that sits on the coffee table in front of me, along with my laptop.

More work.

But I have no parents, no friends, no lover, so work will have to fill this moment.

Atop the pile is the folded summons. Finally (*I know, don't judge me*) I dial the number on the front.

"Salem Court House, how can I direct your call?" the operator asks.

"Yeah, I got a declaration of property delivered, and this number was listed," I say, the vodka slowing my tongue the tiniest bit.

"Please hold for Property," the operator says.

"Okay." I wait.

"Property. What's your case file?" says a gruff voice, who was clearly ready for the workday to be finished.

"Uh ... 675894B," I found it.

"V as in Victor or B as in Bi-noculars?" Gruff asks.

"Binoculars." I hide a laugh.

"Name?" Gruff asks.

"Gray Cooper," I say.

"Ms. Cooper, your case has gone to auction," Gruff says.

"What does that mean?" I say as my heartbeat quickens.

"It means that the assets of Woodman Cooper will be auctioned. Really, you should have called the moment you were served," Gruff says.

"When is the auction?" I ask.

"I'm sorry, we don't have that information. Let me see if there are any notes on which one." Gruff's effort to being helpful.

"Just one note here, and it says, 'Phillips Auction House,' and there is a little asterisk."

"What does that mean?" I ask.

"The asterisk means someone has already called in to claim interest. They move those cases to the top of the docket, to save time. If someone is interested in the lot, it will usually go quickly and keep things moving over there," Gruff says.

"Is there anything I can do to stop it?" I ask.

"Stop the auction? No, that shipped has sailed. Wwwheeeeewww," Gruff whistles.

"But it's my father's office, his things, his paperwork. It's sentimental, who would want it? How did they even know about it?" I say feeling suddenly desperate.

"All property is listed on the city website one week before auction, to keep swift time with the case log. Anything else?" Gruff gruffs.

"No, thanks," I say.

"Have a nice day," Gruff ends the call insincerely.

Looking up the phone number for Phillips Auction House,

as my hands begin to shake. I dial and it rings. Who would have claimed interest in my dad's estate? I can't lose his things. His mugs. They've been my responsibility for less than two weeks, and I'm already going to lose them.

No one picks up.

I down the last sip of vodka and call Joe Nebraska.

14

The Mistwell parking lot is becoming familiar. I stop the car and Joe gets in.

"Howdy," he says.

"Hi." I'm a mess.

"If we rush, we can make it to Phillips Auction House before it closes," he says.

Peeling out of the parking lot, I drive with purpose and speed down Chestnut Street.

"There." Joe points as we nearly pass the small, white sign for the Phillips Auction House. I turn hard and pull Hero into a parking spot, landing perfectly between the lines. Throwing open the door of the car, we rush in to make it before they lock up.

Immediately I start banging on the door, while Joe looks at me surreptitiously. I have little patience.

"Hey, take a breath," he says. Boy do I hate it when he tells me what to do.

Joe eyes me and then the doorknob. He turns it and the door opens easily. I shoot him a look and he shrugs.

A harried receptionist meets us at the door.

"What was all that racket?" she says, appearing formidable.

"Sorry, we have an urgent request and were worried you had already closed," I explain. The woman looks at her watch as she walks back to the tall, wooden counter.

"You have thirty-three seconds – how can I help you?" she asks. I pull the paperwork out of my bag and shove it toward the woman.

"Please, my father's office and all its contents were auctioned off and I need it back. I have the money," I sputter. The woman types into her computer, referencing the papers I've given her.

"You're Gray Cooper?" she asks.

"Yes," I say.

"Okay, well, the records say this palette has been sold and paid for, I'm sorry ma'am." She looks up at me.

My face goes red.

"How? I was *just* served."

"I don't know, ma'am. That's what the record says," she replies unaffected.

"By whom?" I ask. Who could be so interested in my father's old belongings?

"Ma'am, I'm sorry, but that is confidential information," she says.

"But this is my father. I made one late phone call and now you're saying there's nothing to be done?" I'm furious.

"That's right, ma'am," she says.

"Well, can I at least pick up a few things that I left there?" I try, not that I actually left anything in particular.

"No, ma'am, that'd be trespassing," she says. Joe sees my face fill with color and comes over to put his hand gently on my arm and gives it a squeeze.

"Hello, Miss –?" Joe says to her, with swagger.

"Martha," she says, trying hard not to be charmed.

"Miss Martha, I understand that Ms. Cooper here was just minutes too late to save her father's assets from being purchased. Such a shame that we need to process this. I wonder if you could do me a quick favor? We have been running around all day trying to take care of everything, could you spare a cup of water? I'm just parched."

"A cup of water?" Martha repeats.

"I would be in your debt, Miss Martha," he says, and bats his eyelashes a few extra times. There is no way this is going to work. He leans his elbow on the desk, and Martha gets up from her chair and goes to the water jug at the back of the office.

As she does, Joe nods me toward the computer.

I hop up onto the tall counter and lean across, my feet dangling, while Joe keeps his eyes on Martha. I carefully scroll through the records on her screen, looking for the name I so desperately want.

There. Committed it to memory.

Just as Martha turns back, I jump down.

"Bye. Thank you," Joe yells, as I am already out the door. Martha stands in the middle of the office bewildered, holding the cup of water.

I'm sitting in the driver's seat, when Joe reaches the car. He gets in. I look straight ahead.

"Zeke Lassullo," I say.

"Ever heard of him?" Joe asks.

"No," I say. But I thoroughly dislike the taste his name leaves in my mouth.

"That was kind of fun," Joe says.

"Really?" I turn to him.

"Yeah," he says, and his eyes seem to bore through me. I fasten my seatbelt, because I need to restrain myself. My heart is beating in my face. He leans close, like maybe he is going to kiss me. His breath has a hint of mint.

I close my eyes.

"Oh no," he says, and when I open my eyes, I see Martha is storming toward the car with a scowl.

"Shit," I say.

"Go!" Joe shouts, and I back out and leave with much of the same urgency as when we arrived, with a loud peel of the wheels.

Only this time, Joe and I are laughing uncontrollably.

15

Now that I'm banned from my father's office, I can either work at home or find another place. Home feels sad and lonely these days, so I take my work to a café off Main Street called Foam. Foam is tiny; two tables by the window, one outside. Strong coffee and terrible service.

A couple sits at the table outside, and inside there is no one behind the counter. I take a deep breath and look at my watch: it's 3:05 p.m. Taking a seat at one of the tables, I try not to let my mind spin.

Instead, I look out through the glass at the couple, elbows propped with their fanned hands intertwined, while their faces are so close they almost touched. They are deep in conversation, her dark hair ruffled by the breeze. It is such an entangled position, too intimate for being in public, but I can't stop staring, wondering what they are talking about. It looks intense and romantic – maybe she's telling him she loves him for the first time, or maybe he's asking for her to stay this close for always and to never break eye contact or he might just die.

"Sweet, aren't they?" she says, and I turn to see my mother standing behind me.

"Mom," I say breathing in. Every single time she appears, my heart drops and then floats like a fishing bobber.

"Sweetie, how are you?" she asks. I look around to make sure I am still alone.

"Kind of okay, but mostly a mess. What did you mean when you said you started the fire?" I ask quietly, getting to my questions quickly.

"Well, I was trying to get in touch with your father," she says.

"Where? How?" I ask, feeling so worried she will leave again before I can get answers.

"The Incend Ritual. It's... Gray, I know that this has been a lot for you. So much information, in such a small amount of time," she says.

"What is the Incend Ritual?" Can't she just hurry up and tell me everything?

"It's in the book. At first, I thought it was working, I saw Woody," she explains.

"Dad?" I cannot believe she saw him. I haven't seen my father in ten years, and the fact that my mother saw him just a month ago – I can't help the tears.

"I didn't do it properly. Something went wrong, and then I was coughing and coughing until I went to sleep. I'm so sorry," she continues.

"Where is Dad?" I ask.

"He's far from here, not in this reality. I know this will be confusing. He's being held prisoner, but I can't tell you more. I think I've already said—" she says, flickering. She's about to leave.

"No, Mom, who calls you Mads?" I remember to ask. She is fading, her voice a glitched lost call.

"Woo –," she says. Is she saying Woody? Dad? I never heard him call her that. But she is gone.

"You can't sit in here," the thin man behind the counter barks. I'm no longer alone.

"What? Oh," I say, realizing I haven't made a purchase. I wipe my eyes; black mascara stains my hand.

"You can't just sit," he repeats.

"I'm sorry, can I please get a coffee. Black," I say.

The man, whose nametag reads *Kyle*, turns from me swiftly from me to pour the coffee. As I scan the payment code, someone walks in.

Barry Vondale.

"Ms. Cooper," he says. Barry wears an expensive wool coat and looks less sure of himself here. Perhaps when at the Vondale Estate, his confidence is held up by the pillars in front of the mansion rather than by his own person. Kyle eyes him with disdain, waiting to see if he'll order something.

"Vanilla latte with extra sugar," he says and sits at the table by the door. Might as well utilize this run-in.

"Mr. Vondale, funny to find you here."

"I'm meeting someone," he says.

"Oh. I'm working," I say.

"What have you found out about my grandfather?" he asks. I'm not at liberty to tell him anything, but the truth is I don't have much to say.

"Do you think there is a chance he went back to Nevada?" I ask him back. He looks surprised.

"Went back to play cowboys and aliens? Sure, I guess," he says. It's clear that Barry doesn't take his grandfather's work at Area 51 seriously, but it wouldn't hurt to get a bit of intel.

"Did he ever tell you about his work there?" I ask.

"Not really. Mostly he talked to Darby about that stuff. The only story I remember was something about Gramps fighting some alien in the woods and being covered in blue dust. I always remember – how stupid is that – an alien would just throw dust at you? I don't know, I think maybe he did some heavy drugs in those days. Had to, right?" he says.

As Barry speaks about his grandfather's story with complete disgust, I'm reminded of how open-minded and kind Joe was when we talked about it.

"Right, well I should go," I say.

I look down at my bag with my computer and paperwork, and know I have more questions for the other Vondale's.

I leave Foam with my coffee, a story about blue dust and one last glance at the couple in front.

16

When I pull up to the Vondale Estate, I'm relieved no one comes outside to greet me. The house looms with a domineering presence that feels more like a nightmare setting than a home for a family. Tall white joists frame the roof, and the tiny dovecotes in the attic make a face.

A grimace.

I round the corner of the sprawling yard and make my way to the gravel trail Darby mentioned the first time I visited. She told me she had walked the trail, and by now the police have searched it looking for Werner Vondale. Now it's my turn. If there are clues about Vondale or alien abductions, I'll find them.

Fastening the buttons on my trench, I shiver, as it's colder than I expected. The trail is peaceful, the only sound is the crunch of my feet on the gravel and a few birds in the distance. Trees hang over the path and probably make a pleasant cool shade in the summer, but today without the sun, it's ominous.

I try to imagine what he was thinking about life at his age.

Maybe his proximity to death. If he was, I hope it wasn't a premonition.

The leaves have begun to change. Isn't it funny that leaves find their most vibrant colors just before their death? In the spring, they are bright and green and new and hold on through the summer. And then in the autumn, my favorite season, they turn shades of gold, sienna and scarlet. It's like they are shouting to us, look at me in my beauty, just before the trees absorb those nutrient colors and the leaves dry and fall, only to be the food for the next cycle.

I like to think people are like leaves. We spend our youth bright and green, then the farther we move into our adulthood, we bloom into the brighter colors – we learn what's important, we use our beauty to gain knowledge and experience, and at our oldest we share our wisdom with the community. When we die, like a leaf, our energy goes back to the earth and the cycle begins again.

I grab a giant red maple leaf; it's huge. Spreading my hand on top of it, I notice on one of its points something blue.

Blue.

When I examine my hand, there's a small blue smear. Barry Vondale said that Werner fought an alien and got covered in blue dust. He also seemed to think the story was preposterous.

I turn back and find the approximate spot where I picked the leaf up. Searching for more blue, I don't see anything but piles of leaves. There is a thin pathway between two trees, nothing official, looks to be made by the bicycles of children riding the same area over and over.

Carefully, I follow the path off the trail, looking for blue. The path leads to a small clearing with two large rocks, and someone has written KELLIE WAS HERE on the side of one of them. There's a snack-size bag of crackers on the ground. On the far side of the clearing, I see it.

Two mounds of blue dust.

They look like ant hills, and the blue color, though strange, sort of blends with the ground and partial leaf coverage. I can see how the police might have overlooked it.

I take a Ziploc from my bag and gather some of the dust.

It could just be some children playing with chalk or sugar candy, or it might be countless other very normal explanations.

Or Werner Vondale really was abducted by aliens covered in blue dust.

"Gray, is that you?" Darby calls to me. I turn around to find her concerned face, completely bundled in winter hat, she's also wearing mittens and giant puffer coat.

"Just trying to get into the mind of your grandfather, and thought walking the trail would help," I say, putting the Ziploc into my bag.

"What did you find?" she asks, gesturing to the Ziploc.

"It's probably nothing, but I thought I'd have it tested," I say, holding up the bag.

"What is it?" she asks, stepping closer.

"It's blue dust or chalk of some sort. Maybe one of the kids..." I am trying to be nonchalant.

Darby freezes.

This means something to her, and she looks petrified.

"Darby, are you alright?" I ask.

"Yes, fine. It's just a story he used to tell me when I was small and wanting to know about his adventures," she says, suddenly teary.

"Let's walk," I say to calm her, and we start back down the trail toward the house. I jiggle the candy in my pocket.

"You know how I told you about the time when he met an alien?" she says.

"I do," I say.

"Well, there's more to the story that I didn't say, a lot more. I kind of sugar-coated it," she says.

"Tell me the truth."

"When he was sixteen-years-old, he was out in the woods at night, looking for some sort of nocturnal millipede. Instead, he found himself face-to-face with what he called an alien. It was thin and tall, had translucent skin. At first he thought someone from school was dressing up to mess with him. He was bullied a lot, so that would have been nothing unusual. Grandfather said he had been psyching himself up, and promised himself the next time the bullies came for him, he would do something different, he would fight back. And so faced with this strange looking bully at night, he took his walking stick and whacked whoever it was. The bully stared at him, and Grandfather said all the hairs on his body stood on end. The alien opened its mouth wider than any human could and let out a high-pitched sound, and all this blue dust came out," she says.

"It threw up blue dust on your grandpa?" I asked, stifling a laugh. Just like Barry said.

"Yes. He felt pain everywhere in his body. His joints ached, his skin hurt, and he was frozen. He said it hurt more than anything he'd ever felt, and that he was sure he would die. But when the alien closed its mouth, Grandfather took the opportunity to hit it with the stick. He hit it again and again, until it stopped moving. Then he ran home and called the police. Instead of the police from town, he said a black car showed up, and the people who got out wore military gear. Grandfather brought them to where the alien lay on the ground, and then the men took them both to a facility where they did blood and medical tests.

"He kept asking if the kid dressed up as an alien was still

alive. They told him that he didn't make it. Grandfather felt terrible, but they didn't arrest him, they just brought him home and said not to tell anyone about what happened. The men said they would contact him soon.

"When he turned seventeen, they did contact him, they offered him a job with the government at Area 51. He accepted right away. It was a way to escape the jerks at school. He'd become really interested in what happened that night, and he thought he could find out more," she says.

"And did he? Did they confirm it was an alien contact?" I ask, more excited than I thought I would.

"Sorry, Gray, he wouldn't tell me anything that happened at Area 51. He held his nondisclosure in the highest regard," Darby says. Her shoulders relax.

"How did he end up here in Salem?" I ask.

"He met my grandmother when she was on vacation. Dahlia Pershing, heiress to the Pershing fortune. They first lived on Martha's Vineyard with her family, but Grandfather fell in love with lore of Salem, and preferred the conveniences of being off the island. They have many homes, but this place is where we all spend the most time."

Salem was an interesting choice for a man haunted by his time at Area 51. Why not add the witch trials to the mix? We work our way up the path and back to my car.

"Well, I'll get this dust tested and we'll see if it's related to your grandfather at all," I say, feeling more assured it will.

"Gray, what if they took him?" she asks.

"I don't think they did, and no matter what, we'll find him," I tell her. It isn't necessarily true, but she needs to know I'm committed.

17

Using my usual channels to find an address brings me nothing for Zeke Lasullo. *Who are you, Zeke? And what do you want with my father's office?*

Glad to be home, I sit in my coziest chair. I pick up the book *The Paranormal and Their Search for Meaning* and scan the pages, but nothing in it relates to my father. It's all so esoteric, and I'm disappointed it doesn't give me more information relevant to him, about what happened and where he is.

Thinking of Dad being trapped somewhere haunts me.

Gray, you can face reality. I take in a deep breath in and slowly let it out. I can, but later. What if Dad needs me now? It has been ten years, what's a little procrastination?

I can go back and forth all day with myself.

I grab *A Guide for Fit Survival*, flip it open to the first chapter, and actually read it instead of scanning.

READING THE WEATHER

Welcome to your guide to surviving in the Underworld. This chapter will direct you on how to operate under its weather conditions, which will be your first and most important challenge.

The weather in the Underworld is unlike any you will have seen before. It is made up of extremes: fiery heat, polar cold, drowning floods, tsunamis, and bone-cracking thunder. There are a few ways to manage these conditions, even though most will perish upon entrance.

Step 1: Wear goggles. The sulfur rains are your first obstacle. The rain isn't pleasant on the skin, but it won't kill you. However, the acid in this rain will dissolve your eyeballs in seconds. You must keep your eyes closed until the eye of the storm comes and the rain lifts. You know, wait for the eye to keep your eyes. The goggles will act as an added shield and reminder, because every being who has gone without goggles has also gone without eyes from that point forward.

I shut the book.

Besides the terrible attempt at humor, this book is an utter farse. Could he have been trying to go there? Willingly? If he was, why?

Why was my father preparing for the Underworld? Did he go there voluntarily, or did he know he was going to be sent there? How did he know? Who gave him the book? Did it work? I lean my head on the arm of the chair and close my eyes.

My mind swirls into a nightmare. I imagine myself on a dark cliff, standing at the precipice. The sky thunders and the rain comes down. When the acid rain hits my skin it burns, like being attacked by fire ants. And I can't help but open my eyes to be sure I'm not being burned alive. The second I do, my eyes are aflame; I'm blind, and I scream out.

"No," I tell myself, rubbing my arms, assuring myself that I am back home, at my desk.

My phone rings.

I'm hoping it's Joe's contact, who is supposed to call me about testing the blue dust I found. The baggie sits nondescriptly on my shelf.

"Ms. Cooper, I have an address for you," a woman says. Guess not.

"What? Who is this?" I ask.

"This is Laney over at Public Records, you had left a message earlier about someone named Zeke," she says.

"Oh, yes. I'm sorry, go ahead," I say, slowing my breath.

Zeke. An address for Zeke.

"It's 109 Blackbird Plaza, Suite B," she says.

109 Blackbird – that's Dad's office. But Suite B, is the neighboring office – the one that used to share the bathroom. My mind feels like it's hit a wall. The loud noise I heard the other evening... it was Zeke.

He was right next-door.

This means it was *not* a coincidental purchase of my father's estate.

Who the hell is this guy?

I grab my keys and fly out the door.

18

Nighttime in the familiar parking lot somehow feels ominous. Even though I have my pepper spray, I worry what this Zeke person might do. Part of me wants to call Joe for backup, since he seems to be open to helping me with my case. But no, I can handle this on my own.

Multiple cases.

Too many cases.

This one, the case of my father's belongings, could lead to clues regarding his whereabouts. I need to find him. If I can find my father, I won't be an orphan anymore. It would mean I'm not completely alone in this world.

Not alone.

I take a deep breath before pushing open the door to the building. Looking at Suite A, Dad's suite, makes me angrier than I expect. That was *his* office, and it holds *his* things.

Try to be calm, Gray.

But who is this Zeke, anyway? What does he want from Dad? Is he a jilted client or is he after the paranormal information in Dad's files?

No way to know unless you go in.

I knock hard three times on the door for Suite B.

"Enter," I hear a deep, malicious voice call out.

Here goes everything.

When I open the door, it's dark except for a red lamp in the corner giving off Halloween vibes in September. Fits right in, here in Salem. I smell him before I see him, since thick billowing smoke wafts above his desk. Then I see him, jet black hair slicked back, eyes even blacker. He wears a black velour tracksuit and smokes a cigar.

Remember what you're here to do – get your dad's files back.

"Gray Cooper," he says with a spitty rasp.

"Mr. Lasullo, I'm here about the office and files you won at the auction." I cough.

"I know," he says simply.

Reason with him.

"Listen, all the things you purchased were my late father's."

At this he smiles. Who smiles at the mention of someone's dead parent?

"I know," he repeats.

"Oh, you know. Well then, you'll understand that this was all a huge misunderstanding. There is nothing of value in there, only sentimental papers for my family. I'll make sure you are fully refunded with interest, but I'll need you to return the files right away. My family would be so grateful," I explain.

"I'm afraid this is going to be a very quick meeting," he says. I can't read his face but feel his unsettling vibe.

"Okay," I say wearily.

"No," he says as he takes a big inhale from his cigar. *Wait, that's it?*

"No?" I ask, incredulous.

"You heard me," he says. I feel like a child being scolded, and my insides filled with sick.

"Mr. Lasullo, please, those are my files," I beg.

"No, girl. They are mine," he says. Again, with that smile.

Girl.

Girl.

In general, the term doesn't bother me. I use it, and I don't mind if other people use it with respect around me. Yes, "woman" is more accurate, but I was a girl once and that girl is still inside me.

Girls are incredible.

But this guy, he is not using the term with respect; he wants me to feel smaller.

Sorry, Zeke.

This only makes me feel larger, taller, more.

The fury reaches into my chest. My face is turns fifty shades of red, and I want to shove that cigar straight down his throat. Instead, I stand up and step closer to his desk, look him straight in his vacant, black eyes.

"Actually, the office and files belonged to my father," I say smiling, trying a new tactic. "Come on, what do you need them for?"

"They belong to me. I'm not changing my mind," he says.

That's it. This guy has no sympathy for me, it doesn't seem like he has any soft feelings.

"I will get it all back. You fucked with the wrong *girl*," I seethe.

And then I slowly walk out of that office, making sure he hears the rage in each click of my boots.

19

I walk into The Uncanny blazing a trail of fire. The place is already decorated with full macabre enhancement for Halloween. Joe sits in a booth, looking so relaxed in contrast to my intensity. Taking a deep breath, I try to calm down and match his ease, but still pull off my trench with vigor.

"Bad day?" he asks.

"You could say that."

"You met the guy from the auction?" he asks.

"I did," I say, not wanting to recount the story. The anger is still tight on my face, and I'd like a distraction.

"He didn't want to give your father's things back?" he asks.

"How did you know that?" I snip.

He blinks.

Without saying a word, he points out my sour attitude.

Fine, Joe. We don't have to talk about Zeke. Let's talk about Mom.

"How is Mistwell? Did the fire chief call you?" I ask changing the subject.

"It's fine, and he did not. Is this about your mother?" he asks.

"Of course it is," I say louder than I intend to.

"Gray, that case is closed. For now, obviously if you find anything new, let me know. And if the fire chief contacts me with anything to support a theory other than your mother setting the fire, I will listen." He's trying to be gentle.

And I feel guilty, because my mother admitted she set the fire. Well, my ghost mother. *You can't exactly tell him that your ghost mom told you she set the fire, but that she did not kill herself.*

"I'm sorry, it has been a long day," I relent.

"Tell me what happened with Auction Guy," he says.

"The guy Zeke, he was a jerk. He rents or owns the office next to my father's, and I'm not sure about the why yet. I had this creepy feeling, like he knew me and my father, even though I can't find any background info on him at all. Super dismissive too and had no intention of giving me back the files. Money meant nothing to him," I explain.

"Sorry, that sucks," Joe says.

"Thanks. It made me cranky," I say, taking a sip of the water in front of me.

"I like cranky, Gray," he says, leaning closer. I can feel his energy mingle with my own.

"You might regret saying that." I laugh.

"I enjoyed working with you at the auction house, that was the first bit of fun I've had in a while," he says. He's right, the look on the clerk's face standing there with the water was pretty funny.

"That was hilarious," I add.

"Almost as hilarious as you coming into my office when I was naked that one time," he says. My cheeks flush.

"Towel. You had a towel," I remind him. Suddenly, The Uncanny feels warmer and darker.

"Lucky for you," he says.

"Joe, don't flirt with me," I say. *Why did I say that? Because you are not getting into another crash and burn relationship right now. Especially right now.*

"You're right, Cranky," he says, crossing his arms. He looks at me like he is trying to read me. The ice in my veins is melting. Why can't I stop imagining him cooking me pasta and rubbing my shoulders after a long day of PI work?

"Listen, we are not going to end up with each other, so best to quash it now before anyone catches feelings," I say, eviscerating my daydream before he can.

"What if I already have?" he asks.

Oh, no.

"You haven't," I say matter-of-factly.

"How do you know?" He smiles.

"Because you barely know me. You could only possibly have feelings for the idea of me," I say, as I rub my temples, feeling a headache coming on.

"Ouch, I thought we were friends," he says.

We are.

"We can be, but when we know each other better. I have a lot of baggage, Joe," I say.

"Don't we all?"

"Yes, but I've sworn off relationships," I say. *Maybe I should swear off all human interactions in general...*

"Why?" he asks, still not seeming to understand how this whole thing is teetering on the edge.

"Because each one is a part of a cycle I'd rather not repeat – starts great, becomes good, goes off the tracks, and always, always ends in a devastating crash," I say, and take a sip of my water.

"So, you've sworn off experiencing anything fun?" he asks.

Staring down at the table, I wonder if I have, and then looking straight at Joe, I decide.

"I never said that."

We both laugh, releasing whatever weird energy we were conjuring. And because I am feeling punchy, I ask about our last time here at The Uncanny.

"So...you never told me your worst work experience?" I ask. His face constricts. *Hit a nerve. Again. Weird energy reactivated.*

"It's not something I want to talk about right now," he says. He finishes his beer.

"Okay," I say.

Awkward pause. Wow. Whatever it is must be really serious. Why do I always push too far? Go back to the fun.

"Hey, you want to help me get those files back?" I ask. His shoulders relax.

"Now that sounds like my kind of trouble," he says.

20

Back at my place, I change into black jeans, slide on a black tee and black gloves, and tuck my hair under a black beanie.

I'm in my villain era.

Even though Joe sounded interested in helping me get my father's files back, I have reconsidered including him in the part that will technically be a crime. I'm not ready to take on that responsibility.

As for myself?

I don't have much to lose these days.

It won't be hard to break into Zeke Lasullo's office. I know that building.

I park Hero at the cemetery, walk by the haunted gargoyle and then through the small patch of woods that separates the streets. It's getting dark now, and my heart races. The evening is quiet, except for the occasional call of a nearby raven.

It's likely that good ole Zeke has changed the locks, so I don't even try the old key. Instead, I take out my lock pick kit and easily enter my father's office.

A series of beeps tweets the countdown to an alarm.

Shoot.

Didn't expect that.

I shut the door and look around. Nothing has been touched. It looks exactly like it did the last time I was here.

Tweet, tweet, tweet.

We learned in detective school that the standard entry delay on an alarm is thirty seconds, some are sixty seconds. In this case, I err on the side of safety, and I give myself thirty seconds.

Flipping through the options on my device, I find a Wi-Fi alarm kill switch; another detective school gem. To my great relief, it works.

Immediately, I walk over to the bathroom, and try the door, just in case.

No dice.

Taking out my screwdriver, I get to work removing the hinges from the door. As quickly as I can, I remove the bathroom door. It's made of cheap, light wood, and I'm able to lay it down on the floor easily.

Entering Zeke's office gives me the chills. Smells like cigar and old man – not just old – ancient. Something foul and musty.

When I search his desk, I realize I have no idea what I'm looking for.

A clue.

Yes, a clue, that will tell me everything: who he is, and why he's tormenting me. As I shuffle through the first drawer, I hear her.

"Darling, you need to leave," Mom says.

I turn around to find my beautiful apparition of a mother. Her presence is thin this time, as though she's barely made her way into this energy layer.

"Mom, I don't have time for you right now," I say. *How*

could I say this to her? All I want is for her to stay. Please, Mom, stay here forever. Don't leave me.

"Gray, I'm here to tell you to leave. Zeke is bad news," she says. As though I don't already know that.

"I need to find Dad and what happened to you, because apparently you are forbidden to tell me," I snap. I pull papers that have nothing on them out of the desk.

"I'm sorry." She's fading.

"Go, you need to go now."

Usually I would listen to an otherworldly plea to leave a place where a crime is occurring. But it's early evening in a small town, in an office building where nothing remotely bad has ever happened. Besides, I'm already here, it's happening. Now I need something to make it worth the trip.

"Mom, you wouldn't understand, but I'm here – I need to find some proof. Proof that Dad is alive or information on who Zeke is. I just need – a kernel...anything," I say. But Mom has flickered away, back to where she lives now.

The third drawer has files with actual words on them. I recognize the file sticker's with Dad's all-caps handwriting – these are my father's files. He took a stack of my father's files and put them in his desk.

They must be important.

This means something.

As I scan the file folders, one jumps out. It's fat. Hoping it's a file about my father, I take it out. But the name on the file is not his, it's *WERNER VONDALE*.

21

Speed reading the first page, I see it's about young Werner Vondale, at seventeen. This is the case file from when he reported his alien abduction, my father investigated the case. There are photos on the next page. I take photos of them with my phone and text them to myself for backup. Mr. Vondale looks so young and sad. I can see the weight of something heavy in his seventeen-year-old eyes. My heartbeat grows loud in my ears; a reminder to move quickly.

After scanning through all the pages, I put the stack on the desk and move on to the last drawer.

Inside I find a shiny purple stone, with a symbol etched onto it. The stone so pretty, the symbol is a small circle with and s-shape, like a snake. Holding it feels like it's carbonated.

My hand tingles. That's strange.

Crackle. The sound of a car pulling up outside.

I drop the stone in surprise.

I grab the files and shove them back into the desk.

Gingerly, I step over the door and hurry back through the bathroom and back out the front door of my father's office, closing it behind me. I speed down the hallway and duck behind the large trashcan in the lobby.

Someone enters the building.

It's him, I just know it.

Zeke.

My hand tingles like I'm still holding the stone. It's similar to how I feel when Mom leaves. Like I am connected to the energy of something no longer there. It's eerily familiar and feels like magic. Something Dad would know about.

I hear him open his office door and close it behind him.

There will be about fifteen seconds before he notices the bathroom door on the floor.

I bolt for the entrance, and fly out the door, just as I hear him shout something indiscernible.

Jogging for the tree line, I catch the sound of the entry door open, and notice that the raven is quiet now.

Moving like a shadow through the trees and past the gargoyle, and I make it back to Hero, and the only thing that scares me now is the loud sound of her engine.

22

Later that night, after the hottest shower I can stand, I pull on sweatpants and a new tee.

Cozy, at last. I'm still waiting on Joe's guy to get back to me about the blue dust. I'm also waiting on Mom to appear again. Will she keep appearing forever?

I pull a blanket over my shoulders and sink into the couch ready to continue *A Guide for Fit Survival*. It should really be titled *A Guide for the Underworld,* but I suppose that would stand out too much. As I open the cover, there's a knock on my door.

It's 10 p.m.

I can't help but worry it might be Zeke. What if he knows it was me who broke into the office? They knock again, and I rush to the side window to see who it is.

Oh.

I open the door to Joe.

He looks mildly tired, but still the same affable man with the weathered leather jacket.

"Hi, Joe," I say, suddenly self-conscious in my braless sweatsuit situation, my wet hair making big spots of translucent cotton on my shoulders. His gray eyes flicker up, as I cross my arms.

"Sorry, to come by so late, but you forgot this at The Uncanny," he said, dangling my pepper spray.

I grab it.

"Thanks. Uh, you want to come in?" I ask. *Please say no.* Because I definitely will want you to stay and make my life complicated and my bed a mess.

"Yeah, sure," he says.

Opening the door wider, I let him in.

"I'll be right with you, just get yourself some water or something," I say pointing toward the kitchen. I hurry into my room, toss the pepper spray on the bed and quickly grab a bra and struggle it on.

"Nice place. I don't want to bother you, just dropping that off, since I knew you were planning to go see that man again," he says.

After pulling on a hoodie and wrangling my wet hair into a messy bun, I join him in the kitchen.

"Thanks. You didn't have to bring it over though. I could have picked it up," I say.

"I didn't want you to be without a safety device," he says.

"Oh, well I have many. And I should probably tell yo—" I begin. He turns his head as if to hear better.

"Tell me?"

"I already 'went to see that man again,'" I say.

"You did? I thought we were – of course, you did," he says. I smile putting my hands up, trying to lighten the mood.

"I'm sorry. I know, I just didn't want to involve you in anything criminal," I say.

"Criminal? Jesus, Gray, what did you do?" he asks.

I go to the chair where I had dropped the file and handed it to Joe, who has followed me.

"What's this?" he asks.

"One of my dad's case files. It was in Zeke's office," I say proudly.

"And I suppose that Zeke was not there?" he says, looking at me over the file.

"You suppose right, but he did show up and I had to scram before he caught me," I say, my heart beginning to race just remembering how close of a call it was.

"I like that word, *scram*," he says, flipping the pages. "Werner Vondale. This is *the* Werner Vondale?"

"That's the one, the guy I'm trying to locate. He was a client of my father's. So, what do you think? Do you buy it... the aliens?" I ask. He squints at the files, turning the photos around.

"This looks pretty legit," he says, surprised.

"I think so too," I say. It feels good to have someone logical see the proof of something not so logical.

"So, your father was an alien detective?" he asks, his tone too playful.

"No..." I'm defensive, but don't know what to say.

"He investigated alien abductions?" he offers.

"There was a paranormal angle to a lot of his cases, sure, but he was a serious detective," I say.

"I didn't mean to imply otherwise," he says. But he didn't have to. Tears rimmed my eyes, and I can't stop it. The thought of Werner Vondale not being taken seriously, and my dad being made into a joke; it all started to build inside me. And now to have even the slightest bit of insult come from Joe... All the grief I've shoved down starts to rise up, and it scares me.

"You know, I've had a really long day, I think you should go," I say.

"Gray, I'm sorry, I completely– " he tries to explain.

"It's fine, I'm fine, I'm just beyond tired. Thank you for

bringing the pepper spray," I say, standing. Holding the door open, I look down at the floor. I can't let him see this hurt.

I'm not fine.

My sadness and anger are like an active volcano.

"Will you at least look at me?" he asks.

I can't.

Staring harder at the floor, a tear tracing my chin, now I really can't look at him. "I'm sorry. Goodnight," he says.

"Goodnight," I whisper and shut the door.

But my heart is saying, *don't go...*

23

I allow myself to slide down the door and sit on the floor. Well, now I've pushed away my only friend. Why are people so disappointing?

Especially me.

"You are a legacy," my mother says.

"What?" I open my eyes to find my mother sitting next to me on the floor.

"A legacy. Your father was taken from us because he is a powerful source, and I was just not up to the duty of saving him. It wasn't in my blood, I married in," she says.

"Mom, what are you talking about?" I say. Her vague explanations and puzzles are making me as angry as Joe did.

"I'm sorry, I swore to your father I wouldn't tell you for your own safety. But now you must know. You are important, Gray," she says.

"Thanks, but I feel like the most insignificant speck of dust right now," I say.

"Ten years ago, your father was in a fight with a powerful underlord, and in order to protect us...protect you, he made a deal with the devil, as they say," she says.

"What do you mean? Where is he?" I ask.

"He's down there." She points down.

Hell? Does that even exist?

"How do we get him back? I'll go," I say. Mom's face turns a shade of horror.

"No, you absolutely will not. But you do have some power – your legacy. There is a stone. A purple stone," she says. I picture the shining stone, holding it in my hand and feeling it buzzing.

"I know the one. I had it, but I dropped it," I say.

"You've found it? Oh, Gray, you must get that stone back, it will bring you great clarity. If someone else has it, it can be quite dangerous," she says.

"It was in Zeke's office," I say.

Her eyes are pure terror, and she reaches out for me. And fades.

I stare at the place Mom has just been and mark her outline in my mind.

This night has been a disaster, and I know exactly what to do. I go to my speaker and turn on the loudest, hardest music.

I dress in my black bandit outfit again. I am feeling dramatic, so I line my eyes in blackest black, and grab my tactical kit and head back to the office.

No cars again. Lucky me.

This time I have no fear, I'm too full of emotion to be afraid. I'm going to find my father if I have to go to the literal pits of hell to find him.

This time I pick Zeke's office lock, and I have the alarm cut ready, but there's no tweeting. I enter and look around.

No Zeke. Phew.

I see he has leaned the bathroom door against the wall.

Still no alarm.

Interesting.

I get down on the floor with my flashlight, looking for the purple stone, and can't find it at first. Near the desk, I look by the legs and find it. When I pick it up, the stone tingles in my hand again. Mom said it was powerful, and I know that she's right. I feel it. Something inside me has shifted.

I feel powerful.

This criminal behavior is too easy. I smile to myself.

Gray, you are a supervillain.

I pop back up, and rush to the door, stone in hand. As I open the office door, a police officer opens the lobby door at the same time. She is not as surprised to see me as I am to see her.

And then I hear the words no supervillain or novice private detective ever wants to hear –

"You are under arrest."

24

We are in some basement room at the police station. It's been an hour since my arrest, and I'm sitting at a table alone, and the fluorescents are threatening a migraine. They let me make a phone call when I got here, but after leaving Joe four messages, I face the fact that he isn't going to answer.

"Mom?" I call out to no one. She doesn't come.

I swallow carefully, keeping the stone tucked in my cheek. I had immediately pretended to cough and hid it in my mouth when faced with the police. It hums against my cheek.

No one has searched me yet. They just brought me directly to this room. Let me keep my phone.

My arrest is not following proper movie protocol. I'm not sure why. If I'm arrested, this is a strangely open way to treat a criminal. Perhaps they want me to be so comfortable that I confess?

Finally, a woman too young to be in charge of me, comes into the room.

"Gray Cooper."

"That's me," I say.

"I'm Agent Ballist, and we want to talk to you about the Vondale case," she says. Vondale? This wasn't about me breaking and entering Zeke's office?

"ID?" I say. She sighs and slides over a cased ID.

Agent Elenore Ballist. Homeland Security. Oh.

I slide it back across the table. This is one hell of a first case. Sorry, Dad, I didn't mean to bomb so spectacularly.

"We know you have been investigating the disappearance of one Werner Vondale, and we want you to give us what you have," she says.

"What I have? I mean, I don't have much," I say.

"Ms. Cooper, we understand you have been to his house and his workplace. Did you take anything? We need you turn over all evidence you have collected," she states.

"Agent Ballist what does Homeland Security have to do with this?" I ask.

"Classified." Of course.

"What if I tell you this is my case, and I don't want to turn in my evidence to you. Hypothetically," I add.

"Actually... trespassing, breaking and entering, theft... " she lists. So, either I give them my case, or I do actual time in jail and forfeit any chance of a successful business.

"Fine, I'll give you what I have on Vondale. I'm pretty sure he's in Nevada, Area 51. I'm sure you can just call someone and check," I say.

"Oh, we will. You know, the higher up's are impressed with you for some reson, Ms. Cooper," Agent Ballist says.

"And how do the higher ups know anything about me?" I ask, feeling exposed.

"Classified. But don't look at this as losing a case, it can be mutually beneficial," she says.

I'm not sure how, but I surrender.

"Come with me," she says.

I follow her up the stairs and out.

She drives me home so she can take the files I've got on Werner Vondale.

Maybe they'll find him faster, and part of me is relieved for Darby.

Agent Ballist takes everything: she takes my father's files and transfers the pictures on my phone to hers before deleting everything on my device.

She also takes the blue dust.

25

This morning, I'm meeting Darby at Foam because I can't get enough of their sour barista Kyle. I immediately order my coffee, to avoid his wrath.

"You said it's important," Darby says, sitting at a table.

"Good news and bad news," I say. Even if it is bad – bad for me.

"Alright," she says, preparing herself.

"Darby, I can't continue on this case," I say.

"No."

"But it's only because the federal government is taking over. And while I'm annoyed that they took my dad's file on your grandfather and all my notes and evidence, it really is best for you because they have much greater resources than I do. I'm sure they'll find him quicker than I could," I say regretfully.

"You promised," she says, looking betrayed.

"I didn't really have a choice."

"Well, if you think they'll move more quickly?"

"I do. They'll find him, I can feel it," I say. When all I really feel is bitter and apologetic.

"Thank you, Ms. Coo – Gray," she says, and hugs me.
"Thank you for trusting me, but they'll find him," I say.
I hope I'm not making another false statement.

26

Feeling like everything has been taken from me, all that is left is my sorrow and regret. Trying to make amends is the only thing for me to do.

I find Joe at The Uncanny, sitting in the same seat at the end of the bar like the first time we met here. Trivia night. But tonight it's quiet, only a handful of patrons.

REM plays as Rooster pours me a vodka on ice.

Sitting next to Joe, I feel that familiar peace he emits.

"Howdy," he says, more quietly than usual.

"I'm sorry, Joe," I tell him.

"For what?" he asks.

"For being a complete disaster machine," I say, trying to laugh.

"Gray, you are ... you are not," he says.

"I got arrested," I say.

"I know. You left me fifty-seven messages, remember? I'm only sorry I lost my phone and just got to listen to those gems this afternoon. Who knew you were such a criminal mastermind," he says.

"Hardly. I've kind of lost everything." My voice cracks on the last word, and I take a sip of my drink.

You are not going to cry right now.

He rests his hand on my arm.

"You haven't," he says.

"The Feds took over the Vondale case, Zeke took over my father's office, my mom is dead." The tears are coming, so I change the subject. "Sorry, how have you been? How did you lose your phone?" Thankfully, he sees what I'm doing and allows me the distraction.

"Ocean. Yep, don't ask," he says.

We laugh.

"Good one," I say, trying to gain back some composure.

"Did you know I used to be a 9-1-1 operator?" he asks.

"I did not. Wow, that seems like a difficult job," I say.

"Difficult, yes, but I loved it. I felt like I was actually helping people. I mean, there is no greater equalizer than when a person needs help," he says. It's true.

"I'll bet you were great at it," I say.

"No. I mean, I tried to be, but no, in the end I was terrible at it. See, I got this one call. A little girl, Allison, nine years old, called in. She was home alone with her younger brother, four, when she fell down the stairs and onto a shoe bench, and piece of the wood pierced her back. She was so smart. Had her brother bring her the phone and called us. She said there was a lot of blood.

"When she told me the address, I knew it would take an ambulance twelve minutes to get there. I was less than five minutes walking distance away. It's against the law for operators to interfere on a call in any way. But she was a baby, and they were so close. I tried to keep her distracted by asking her about school and her mother, who was at work at the laundromat. But her speech slowed, and I knew we were losing her," he says.

"Oh my god," I gasp.

"So, I hung up and ran faster than I ever have – got to the address three minutes later. I banged on the door, but it was locked. It took her little brother a few minutes to open the door, but when I got to Allison, she was gone." He put his face in his hands.

"Oh, Joe," I say, rubbing his back.

He sits up, takes a swig of his beer, and a deep inhale.

"Of course, they fired me. But every year, I go to the cemetery on Ocean Street and pay my respects. That's where I was when I lost my phone. And, uh, that was my worst moment at work," he says. Now I feel like a heartless jerk for pressuring him to tell me at that stupid trivia night.

"God, I'm so sorry that happened to you," I say. "Being human is some serious shit."

"Right?"

"Thanks for sharing that with me." I think we're definitely friends now. It's like a little trust bud grew.

And so, I decide to tell him.

"I have something I want to tell you, too... My mother is a ghost," I say.

His eyebrows shoot up, he swallows hard.

"I know, probably not exactly what you expected me to say, but I assure you that I'm of sound mind. You know how my dad worked in the paranormal – well, it's kinda like that," I say.

"So, you see her?" he asks.

"See her, hear her, miss her, all of the above," I say. He hugs me and I hug him back. And that's how we leave it.

27

I drive out to the beach, and the ocean air is cool and salty. I haven't been back to Mom's bench since the funeral. I need to talk to her, and she hasn't visited. Bringing the purple stone from Zeke's office, I roll it around in my hand.

"Mom," I say over and over in my mind and out loud.

But she doesn't come.

"Okay, well, if you're not going to appear, I'm just going to talk to you. Because maybe you're not real anyway. Perhaps you are just a figment of my imagination, something I conjured up because I miss you. Because I do, so fucking much. I know, no cursing, Gray, you sound like a pirate. I don't care.

"You were the one person I knew would always be there, to give advice or a hug or even just to tell me off. I have known you the longest of anyone else in my whole life; I was never here on this Earth without you. Until now. It feels like I'm missing a piece of my foundation. What do I do without a foundation, Mom?

"How am I supposed to do life now? I was pretty bad at it

with you here, and now it just feels like a lost cause." The tears are sheets on my face.

"Gray Melodias," she says, "always so dramatic."

"You came," I cry.

"Yes," she says.

"Mom, I don't know how to do this," I say, squeezing the stone.

"Do what?"

"Life. Work. Be a person, have relationships with people."

"You're doing it just right. The messier the better. Just be you, Gray, and trust your instincts. Be careful, but also be careless sometimes. No one knows anything. Not me, not your father. Look at this wild legacy we've left you. I'm sorry and I miss you too," she says.

"Who am I?" I ask. Desperate for clarity.

"While I can't completely answer that, I can tell you that you have a special connection to the other worlds. Your father had it, and so do you. I'm just a try-hard outsider, but you have the power to help people, and not just regular people, but those in the supernatural," she says.

Oh, so now she tells me I'm meant to be a pariah like Dad. I hate to admit that I know she is right. I've always felt it, this connection to otherworldly things, sensations about people both dark and light.

"What does that mean practically?" I ask.

"It means that you are meant to be like your father – to investigate, to be a helper to those cast out by society, to those not known in society. To the paranormal, some call it," she says.

"I can't even solve my first case," I say, wallowing.

"There will be so many more cases," she says.

I couldn't even solve yours.

"Mom, what happened with the fire?" I ask her with finality.

"I was attempting to rescue your father. The Incend Ritual. You can find it in *The Witches Almanac*. He was there, his face became clear. And then something went wrong, and a spirit materialized from the spell, and strangled me. The fire got out of control and moved beyond the ritual area. I was coughing and coughing, and it all went black," she tells me.

"And the letter?" I say, thinking of the proof that started this whole thing.

"What letter, darling?" she asks.

"The one that said, 'please forgive me' and that you messed up and everything went up in flames, the letter that Mistwell used to confirm that your death was not an accident," I told her. My hands describing it more than my voice.

"Oh, that. It was a letter to your father. I was explaining how all my rescue attempts had failed. I needed to tell him that things were getting more serious with George, and I hoped he'd forgive me for moving on. I was just so desperately lonely, Gray. The last time I had tried the ritual, it started a small fire, and believe me, I did not expect future attempts to be worse than that one. I took every precaution. How naïve I was, I'm sorry to you both. Will you ever forgive me?" she asks.

Her remorse and sadness reach me through all the layers of her being. I had no idea she felt so much guilt about George, since their relationship had happened so organically. George made her laugh, after years of sadness and grieving. I hold no ill will toward her for it. And she was trying to save my dad. Her altruism is such a big part of who she is, and it is quite aligned for her to have died in that way.

"Of course I do, Mom." I reach for her, but only meet air.

"A shame I didn't complete the ritual in time, I was so close," she says. It all sounds horrible.

"Mom, what a terrible way to go," I say.

"I didn't feel a thing," she says. Hearing this gives me such clarity on how much she loved my dad. She didn't give up on him, even though she had George. She sacrificed herself to save Dad. It was a macabre love story, but a love story all the same. Either way, Dad is still trapped.

"The ritual. I can do it," I told her.

"No. Absolutely not. You don't want to end up like me," she warns.

"You said be messy. I'm going to get Dad back," I say.

Her image wavers.

"I love you," she says.

And like she always does, she flickers away.

"I love you, too," I say to the wind.

28

Driving in the black of night, the music blaring I feel a little free. Something inside me may have healed. It's funny how that can happen – one moment you're feeling the worst of it, and the next you remember with starry eyes how precious this life truly is.

I look up at the sky, wondering if Werner Vondale has really gone on an alien adventure or if he's just gone for a long walk like his family keeps saying. The file said he killed an alien. What if more of its kind came back for revenge? What if they wanted an explanation? I can understand that.

My phone lights up the darkness. It's Agent Ballist.

"Gray Cooper?"

"That's me," I say.

"Out of respect for your case, I'm calling to inform you that Werner Vondale was just found on the baseball diamond at Salem High," she said.

Wow, she respects my case.

"Is he alive?" I ask.

"Alive," she says.

"Thank you for letting me know. What hosp– " I start to ask.

Click.

29

The doorway at Mistwell Insurance is decorated with Christmas lights. So festive, and I can't help but wonder if it was Joe or Blake's doing.

On second thought, definitely Joe.

He's a softy underneath the leather, but I'll bet he made Blake hold the hooks.

The bell rings as I walk through the entrance. He must've heard my car because Joe has already opened the door to his office.

I walk over.

"So, Joe." I look at the floor and then up at him leaning in the doorway, like he always does.

"So, Gray." He smiles. "I have some good news."

"You do? Tell me," I say, boosting myself up to sit on the counter by Blake's desk.

"Your mother's cause of death is going to be changed to accidental," he says. I clasp my hands.

"What?" I say, shocked.

"I talked to the fire chief, and he agrees that there is room for interpretation on that letter. George came down and made a statement confirming he witnessed your mother writing the letter to your father, well before the fire," Joe says.

"He did? Holy smokes, Joe, thank you." I can't believe it. He cleared my mother. I hop back down and hug him.

He doesn't let go, so I break the embrace.

"Well, in light of this good news, I have a proposition for you," I begin.

"I'm in," he says before I can ask.

"You can't be 'in,' I haven't even told you what *it* is," I say.

He laughs.

"Listen, Gray, ever since you walked into my office and started turning me down left and right, I've had a feeling about you. And these last few weeks have been the wildest and brightest I've had in years. I think if you asked me to fly to Saturn with you, I would," he says with a sincerity not lost on me. I squeeze my hands tightly together, because, without compare, that is the kindest thing anyone has ever said to me.

And I know he means it; it's not just a worn cliché he tatted out easily. With all my emotions rushing to the surface, I grab one of his hands, hoping to stem the flood of feelings I've caught and tell him how I happy I feel.

Instead, I ask, "Why Saturn?"

"I don't know, it has those rings," he says spinning a finger in the air.

"Joe, will you be my partner?" I say softly.

"What's that?" Joe stands up straight, his eyes shining. Our hands still clasped, he grips tighter.

"Strange Investigations. Will you work with me in my business as a PI?" I ask, worried he might think I mean something else. Carefully I tuck my hand away.

"You've got to start somewhere," he says.

"Is that yes?"

"Yes."

Just like that.

"Thank you. I mean, you wouldn't have to leave Mistwell, only help out on cases you have time for. And I'll pay you, of course," I say, rapid fire.

"Wow, yeah. Like I said, I'm in," he says, running his hands through his hair. And then he pulls me in close, and I let him, resting my head on his shoulder.

"You better be ready. I mean we could potentially find ourselves on the rings of Saturn," I joke.

Joe parts from our hug, puts his hands on my shoulders. It feels like he might kiss me again.

I breathe in.

Instead, he puts his hand out for a handshake, which surprises me. I suppose this is what business partners do.

"To the rings of Saturn."

He didn't expect my firm handshake.

"The rings of Saturn," I return.

In these terrible, grief-stricken times, knowing I can't keep seeking relief in the wrong places, this is one thing I can hold on to. Joe is here, and willing to go on this journey with me, and even if it feels complicated, this one time in my life I want to follow my instincts, like my mom said.

The paranormal, the risk of owning my own business, the family secrets already revealed and yet to be revealed, my feelings for Joe – all of it.

I'm just going to run forward holding onto the only thing I know is mine: my intuition.

"I know the perfect place to secure an office space, *and* it won't affect your commute at all," I say.

30

I'm sitting in an idling Hero, with the window open. I'm not sure why I've come here. I think I'm a glutton for punishment. Last night ended on a high, so here I am back in the darkness.

Staring at the bland building that houses what used to be my dad's agency, I think about that first meeting with Zeke and how smug he was. It's funny how someone behaving badly can nudge you into growth.

I'm going to get my father and his files back. And this guy Zeke, is only serving as a catalyst to my doing so. I've never been so sure that I need to pursue detective work.

Paranormal detective work. It's in my blood.

Suddenly, a throbbing sensation hits my head. It's a strong pressure, like something is trying to wrestle itself into my consciousness. An instant headache.

Instinctively, I grab the purple stone from my cupholder, and flip it over in my hand. The pulsing stops.

I hear an echo. *Gray.*

"Gray, go. You need leave now," I hear my mother. I survey the car, but she's not there.

"Mom?" I ask the air.

"Go." It's my mother's faded voice.

Just then, the lobby door of the building swings open, and the billow of smoke announces him before I even see him. The stone buzzes in my hand.

Zeke.

He stands in the doorway, staring menacingly.

Like he can see through my bones.

It takes every bit of self-restraint I have not to put the car in drive and aim at his sadistic face.

I stare back. Crushing the stone in my hand, it's sending electricity through my arm.

I put Hero in drive, leaving hot rubber in my wake.

This isn't over, Zeke.

I promise.

31

Agent Ballist called this morning, while I was recovering from my Zeke headache, and told me that Werner Vondale is at Salem Heights Hospital.

I clutch the bouquet of corner-store flowers too tight.

I'm nervous.

I hate hospitals. The sweet and sterile scent reminds me of the night my mother died.

At the nurses' station, I give them room 433 for Werner Vondale. They point me down the hall.

Darby greets me at the door. Two agents dressed like Ballist sit inside.

"He's asleep," she says. I hand her the flowers.

"Thank you. Let's go sit in the cafeteria. You can say hello when he wakes," she says. There is a sparkle in her eye, like the photos from when she was young on display at the Vondale Estate.

"I can't believe he said he was abducted," I say.

"He said he was able to make amends with them, and that's why he was returned," she says. I follow her down the hallway.

"Fascinating," I say. It truly is.

"He has some pretty unbelievable stories, and he's so happy that his old unit at Area 51 want him to come back and share his experience," she says.

"That's great, Darby. I wanted to let you know something has been bothering me about your grandfather's case."

"What?" she asks.

"That life insurance money being left to your brothers'," I say.

"Oh, right," she says, her face dropping.

"I figured it out."

"Why did he do it?"

"Basic answer – it's an old policy. He had that policy drawn up before you and Caroline were born," I say.

A smile spreads across her face.

"Of course. I can't believe I was worried Grandfather was secretly their biggest fan," she's relieved.

"Glad I could clear that up." I laugh.

"Even better, he's asked me to move out to Nevada with him. Help take care of him and have some adventures of my own. YOLO, right?" she says. Darby is nearly bouncing.

"Sounds fun, I'm really happy for you," I tell her, because I am.

"Gray, I want to thank you for everything."

"I only wish I could've done more."

"You found the blue dust, you proved he was abducted, and now he gets to enjoy the respect he has always deserved."

I knew I would like this job.

32

It's mid-morning, the sun warming the frost on my windshield. I pull Hero into the parking lot in front of Mistwell Insurance.

Joe sits blindfolded in the passenger seat. His soft breath is a comfort.

I help him out of the car and guide him gingerly down the sidewalk, leading him in the opposite direction from Mistwell. I put my hands on his shoulders, pulling him to a stop. Slowly, I peel off the blindfold, as we stand in front of the shop door where the new sign reads:

Gray Cooper & Joe Nebraska, Strange Investigations. It's presumptuous. I'm presumptuous. All I can do now is present it with my honest enthusiasm. I stand holding my hands in a ta-da pose.

He slow-claps.

"What do you think of the font?" I ask, unsure. I'm always unsure of fonts. I know what I don't like, but the ones I do like become a mash-mash in my brain, and then I start to doubt if I like it at all.

"Looks incredible," he says crossing his arms.

But he isn't looking at the sign, he's looking at me.

Something rolls inside me.

"None of this would be possible without that insurance money. Come and see inside," I say, regaining my giddiness.

When I open the door, I'm shocked to find a thin man wearing Ray-Bans sitting at the front desk. *Who let him in here?*

Nothing ever goes the way I expect it to.

"Can I help you?" I ask, looking at Joe with *I-don't-know-this-man* eyes. Joe moves closer to me, his arm grazing mine.

"Are you Gray Cooper?" he responds. His bright white teeth showing.

"I am," I say, taking a breath.

"Thank gods," he says. "I heard you help people of the um, mystical sort?"

How do I have a reputation already?

"Maybe," I say. "What do you mean by mystical?"

The man stands up, he's tall; a long black cape falls to the floor from behind his bomber jacket. As he assumes his full stature, his kind, wise eyes gleam, and his smile is sort of irresistible.

"My name is Conrad, I'm a ... vampire, and I'm being framed," he says, his smile fading into desperation.

I let his words sink in.

"Okay, Conrad, just ... um, stay here, and give us a minute?" I ask.

"Yes, sure," he says, wringing his hands.

Taking Joe's hand, I pull him back outside the office and shut the door.

I hold myself back from running to Hero, driving home, climbing into bed and pulling the covers over my head until I become an old woman.

"Am I mad, or did he just say vampire, because I'm pretty sure that's what I heard?" I ask, wide-eyed.

"I think he did, but the madness is up for debate," Joe says with an easy smile. He seems completely calm about the fact that there is a vampire in the new office.

This is it. This is exactly why I made him my partner: he is the serene water to my choppy waves.

"I guess this is what I signed up for," I say.

Joe nods.

I straighten my shirt, clear my throat, and reenter my new office with authority.

ACKNOWLEDGMENTS

So grateful to all of the podcast listeners of The Strange Chronicles, it always blows my mind to hear that people listened besides my friends and sister. This book series is tribute to the characters developed for that show.

This book wouldn't be possible without the thoughtful contributions of Savannah, Brad and Two Birds Author Services.

Thank you to my family and friends for the encouragement.

Chris, thank you for producing The Strange Chronicles podcast and your support for these stories. Boys, follow your dreams, especially the ones you question.

Readers, this is for you.

ABOUT THE AUTHOR

Jennifer Lauer is the author of THE GIRL IN THE ZOO and THE STRANGE CHRONICLES: START SOMEWHERE, known for her distinctive blend of emotional depth and science fiction. Her writing explores the complexities of human relationships through the lens of speculative themes. The BookLife Prize praised her work – "While the topic of artificial intelligence is familiar territory in fiction, Lauer's work feels especially original, riveting, and timely."

In addition to her novels, Lauer also writes for television and film, and has a podcast called THE STRANGE CHRONICLES. Lauer continues to carve out a unique space in genre fiction with her emotionally resonant storytelling.

ALSO BY JENNIFER LAUER

THE GIRL IN THE ZOO (2023)

AFTERWORD

If you enjoyed this book and want to be updated on the next in the series and learn more about my other work —

Please follow my instagram:
 @jenniferleelauer and
 join my free newsletter The Delicate Papers here:

Printed in the USA
CPSIA information can be obtained
at www.ICGtesting.com
LVHW090216031124
795418LV00007B/915